PICTORIAL
METAMORPHOSES
AND OTHER FANTASIES

Books by Hermann Hesse

Pictor's Metamorphoses

AND OTHER FANTASIES

HERMANN HESSE

Edited, and with an introduction, by
THEODORE ZIOLKOWSKI

Translated by
RIKA LESSER

Farrar, Straus and Giroux
New York

Farrar, Straus and Giroux
19 Union Square West
New York 10003

The Library of Congress has catalogued the hardcover edition as follows:
Hesse, Hermann, 1877–1962.
    Pictor's metamorphoses, and other fantasies.
    Contents: Lulu (1900) — Hannes (1906) — The merman
(1907) — The enamored youth (1907).   I. Ziolkowski, Theodore.
II. Title.
PT2617.E85A6   1982
833'.912   81-12616
AACR2

Contents

*The year of composition follows each title; in most cases,
first publication in German also occurred that year*

Introduction

IN AN AUTOBIOGRAPHICAL SKETCH entitled "Childhood of the Magician" (1923), Hermann Hesse confessed that it had been his overriding ambition, while he was a child, to become a magician. This ambition stemmed from a dissatisfaction with what people conventionally call reality. "Very early I felt a definite rejection of this reality, at times timorous, at times scornful, and the burning wish to change it by magic, to transform it, to heighten it." In his childhood, the wish was directed toward external childish goals —to make apples grow in winter or to fill his purse with gold and silver. Looking back, however, Hesse came to realize that his whole subsequent life had been motivated by the desire for magic powers—though by magic he now meant the transformation of reality, the creation of a wholly new reality, in his writing.

Certainly the distrust of everyday "reality"—it is characteristic that he customarily bracketed the term with quotation marks to indicate what he regarded as its tentative, problematic nature—remained a conspicuous theme in Hesse's thought throughout his life. In 1930 he wrote to a reader: "I don't believe in our politics, our way of thinking, believing, amusing ourselves; I don't share a single one of the ideals of our age." Ten years later he stated in another letter that "it is becoming apparent that the so-called 'reality' of the technologists, the generals, and the bank directors is growing constantly less real, less substantial, less probable."

At the same time, Hesse inevitably coupled his rejection of present "reality" with an assertion of his faith in a higher truth. "I am not without faith," he continued in the letter of 1930. "I believe in laws of humanity that are thousands of years old, and I believe that they will easily outlive the turmoils of our times." In 1940 his denial of "so-called reality" concluded with the claim that "all spiritual reality, all truth, all beauty, all longing for these things, appears today to be more essential than ever."

This perceived dichotomy between contemporary "reality" and eternal values produces the tension that is characteristic of Hesse's entire literary oeuvre. The heroes of his best-known novels—Demian, Siddhartha, Harry Haller of *Steppenwolf*, Goldmund, H.H. in *The Journey to the East*, and Joseph Knecht, the magister ludi of *The Glass Bead Game*—are men driven by their longing for a higher reality that they have glimpsed in their dreams, their visions, their epiphanies, but tied by history and destiny to a "reality" that they cannot escape. At times, however, Hesse sought to depict that other world outright, and not simply as the vision of a figure otherwise rooted in this world.

Northrop Frye has observed that "fantasy is the normal technique for fiction writers who do not believe in the permanence or continuity of the society they belong to." Accordingly, fantasy is the appropriate generic term for

Introduction

Hesse's attempts—both in his fiction and, as we shall see, in his painting—to render the world of which his fictional surrogates can only dream. In his classic essay "On Fairy-Stories" (1939), Tolkien defined fantasy as "the making or glimpsing of Other-worlds," and many of Hesse's works display precisely the "arresting strangeness," the "freedom from the domination of observed fact," that Tolkien has elsewhere called the essential qualities of fantasy. But fantasy, as the tension between an unsatisfactory "reality" and an ideal reality suggests, is more than the creation of other-worlds *per se*. A more precise definition might specify that fantasy is a literary genre whose effect is an ethical insight stemming from the contemplation of an other-world governed by supernatural laws.

By far the most common form of fantasy practiced by Hesse was the fairy tale or, to use the somewhat broader German term, the *Märchen*. Symptomatically, his earliest extant prose composition was a fairy tale entitled "The Two Brothers" (included here in the piece called "Christmas with Two Children's Stories"). In this *Märchen* from the pen of the ten-year-old Hesse, a crippled child runs away from home because he is despised by his strong and handsome older brother. Arriving in the mountains, he is adopted by the dwarfs who mine diamonds there. Years later, the older brother, having lost the use of his right arm in the wars, wanders into the mountains. Meeting his brother, whom he fails to recognize, he begs a crust of bread. The younger brother leads him into the cave and offers him, instead, all the diamonds that he can dig out by himself. When the one-armed beggar is unable to extract a single jewel, his host says that he would gladly permit the man's brother to assist him. Thereupon the beggar, breaking into tears, admits that he once had a brother, small and crippled yet good-natured and kind, whom he had callously driven away. At this display of remorse, the younger brother discloses his identity, and the two brothers live happily together ever after.

When he analyzed this bit of juvenilia many years later, Hesse noted that it was based not upon his own experience —he had never wittingly seen a diamond, much less a mountain of jewels inhabited by dwarfs—but upon his reading, notably the Grimms' *Fairy Tales* and the *Arabian Nights*. These two collections, with which Hesse became acquainted as a child, remained his favorites throughout his lifetime. In 1929 he singled out the *Arabian Nights* for inclusion in his ideal "Library of World Literature," calling it "a source of infinite pleasure." Although all the peoples of the world have produced lovely fairy tales, he continues, "this classic magic-book suffices for our library, supplemented solely by our own German *Märchen* in the collection of the Brothers Grimm."

Hesse was not simply stating the obvious on the basis of limited knowledge; he knew what he was talking about. In an extended career of book reviewing, he appraised many collections of fantasies from countries all over the world, including Richard Wilhelm's edition of Chinese fairy tales, a translation of Somadeva's folktales from India, a twelve-volume set of Oriental tales, Enno Littmann's anthology of Arabian *contes des fées* from Jerusalem, Leo Frobenius's edition of African folktales, and Douglas Hyde's volume of fairy tales from Ireland. He welcomed new editions of Musäus's classic anthology of German folktales as well as Andersen's fairy tales. He recommended Friedrich von der Leyen's international collection of *Märchen* along with an anthology of the world's finest fairy tales, edited by his friend Lisa Tetzner, who was well known in the twenties as an author and reciter of *Märchen*.

Hesse was not merely a connoisseur of fairy tales; he also understood something about their history and theory. He knew that folktales employ a limited stock of familiar motifs that recur in constantly varying configurations, and he was aware of the Oriental sources of many European tales as well as the ancient sources of many medieval tales. Fairy tales, he wrote in 1915 (in an essay on "German Storytellers"), are documents that reaffirm "the eternally identical structure of the human soul in all peoples and all lands." The fairy tales of the world provide us with incomparably valuable examples of "the genetic history of the soul."

In the light of this predilection, it is hardly surprising that Hesse undertook, from time to time, to write *Märchen* of his own—works in which the techniques and motifs of the international repertoire of fairy tales are much in evidence. At first glance, this fascination seems predictable in a writer who often asserted his fondness for Oriental culture and German romanticism, two of the principal sources for the fairy tales of the world. Yet we must not take too much for granted. Why, to put it most simply, does a mature writer in the twentieth century write fairy tales?

We can start with Hesse's thoughts. When he compared his early story "The Two Brothers" with a similar tale written some sixty years later by his grandson, Hesse observed that in both cases a wish is magically fulfilled, and in both cases the narrator has constructed for his hero a role of moral glory, a "crown of virtue." In short, both tales are characterized by elements of the supernatural (magical wish fulfillment) and by an explicit ethical dimension.

We see precisely the same pattern underlying Hesse's most entrancing fairy tale, "Pictor's Metamorphoses." When Pictor first enters the garden of paradise, he is captivated by the continual transformations that all nature is undergoing: he sees a bird turn into a flower, the flower into a butterfly, and the butterfly into a colored crystal with magical powers. Before he has fully comprehended the laws of transformation, yet eager to become a part of that wonderful process, he seizes the magic stone and overhastily wishes to be transformed into a tree. After his metamorphosis, Pictor realizes that he is still not part of the cycle of transformation because, unlike all the other creatures in the garden, he has remained single, he is not a pair. Hence he is doomed to retain a specific form. Many years later a young girl comes into the garden, picks up the stone, and is transmuted into the tree along with Pictor. Now, in their new unity, they undergo transformation after blissful transformation. In other words, the device of double wish fulfillment is used to illustrate a moral situation: the first wish creates the plight which is subsequently resolved by the fulfillment of the second wish. Hesse is also capable of using the elements of the *Märchen* for purposes of humor or irony. In "Tale of the Wicker Chair," a talking chair precipitates the ethical insight: a young dilettante has been inspired by reading a biography of Van Gogh to try to paint the simple objects in his garret. When he discovers how difficult it is to paint even a wicker chair, he decides to give up painting for what he considers the easier job of writing. In a later *Märchen* it is suggested that "Bird" may be the bird from "Pictor's Metamorphoses"; but he is also an allegorical projection of Hesse himself, who was known to his third wife by the nickname *Vogel* ("bird"). At first regarded fondly as a queer eccentric by the inhabitants of Montagsdorf (Monday Village, a pun on Montagnola, the Swiss village where Hesse lived), "Bird" is eventually driven away when a price is put on his head by foreign governments and the villagers begin to shoot at him. Again we find the magical transformation—which psychoanalysis calls a theriomorphic projection—that gives rise to a heavily allegorical tale with pronounced ethical implications. Indeed, the whole tale is very lightly veiled autobiography. But here Hesse has added a further ironic twist. After Bird's disappearance, various legends begin to circulate about him. "Soon there will be no one left who can attest that Bird ever actually existed." Future scholars will no doubt prove, Hesse suggests, that the legend is nothing but an invention of the popular imagination, constructed according to folkloristic laws of mythmaking. Here Hesse uses the form of the *Märchen* to make an ironic comment on the academic study of fairy tales, which tends through its analysis to disenchant the very object of its study, as well as the scholarly assessments of his own works, to several of which he alludes playfully in the text.

In every case, then, from the fairy tale of the ten-year-old Hesse to the ironic fable of the sixty-year-old, the narratives that Hesse specifically labeled as *Märchen* display two characteristics that distinguish them from his other prose narratives. There is an element of magic that is taken for granted: wish fulfillment, metamorphosis, animation of natural objects, and the like. And this magic incident produces in the hero a new dimension of ethical awareness: the necessity of love in life, the inappropriateness of ambition, and so forth. To be sure, wonders and miracles occur in other forms of fantasy employed by Hesse: but elsewhere the miracle is regarded as an interruption or suspension of normal laws. In the legends, for instance, the miracle represents an intervention by some higher power (e.g., "The Merman" or "Three Lindens") that underscores the special nature of the occurrence. The figures in the fairy tales, in contrast, accept the wonders as self-evident: they do not represent any intrusion of the supernatural into the rational world, because the entire world of the *Märchen* operates according to supernatural laws. Little Red Riding Hood takes it for granted that the wolf can talk; the wicked stepmother in "Snow White" consults her magic mirror just as routinely as a modern woman might switch on her television set; and the tailor's son is not astonished at a table that sets itself with a feast when the proper formula is uttered. Hesse's *Märchen* share this quality of self-evident magic. Pictor does not question the powers of the magic stone; the aspiring young artist is not astonished when the wicker chair talks back to him.

However, a world in which magic is taken for granted does not in itself suffice to make a fairy tale: it must also be a world with an explicit ethical dimension. Oversimplified interpretations have argued that the world of fantasy is one in which things happen in accord with the expectations of naïve notions of good and evil, right and wrong. More sophisticated theorists offer a different explanation: the fairy tale begins with a situation of ethical disorder and finally, after resolving the conflicts, reestablishes a new order. Still others regard the *Märchen* as the poetic expression of man's confidence that we live in a meaningful world. All the theorists agree that the supernatural events do not occur simply for the delectation of the reader or listener; rather, the fairy tale reminds us through its magic that despite all appearances to the contrary there is meaning and order in the world. As Bruno Bettelheim points out in *The Uses of Enchantment*, "the child can find meaning through fairy tales," which offer an experience in moral education through which he brings order into the turmoil of his feelings. This is precisely the message of Hesse's *Märchen*: the characters are brought to an awareness of some principle of meaning that they had previously misunderstood. Indeed, the ethical dimension is

(xv

pronounced in all fantasies, whether or not they display the explicitly supernatural element that characterizes fairy tales.

The impulse toward fantasy remained powerful in Hesse's temperament throughout his life. The fairy tale of "The Two Brothers" was written in 1887, when he was ten years old; "The Jackdaw" was a product of his seventies. Between those two extremes, the various forms of fantasy that Hesse employed reflect accurately the stages of his development as a writer. "The Two Brothers," as Hesse recognized, was patterned closely after the so-called *Volksmärchen*, or popular fairy tales, that he knew as a child from the collection of the Brothers Grimm. His later fantasies are more profoundly indebted to the so-called *Kunstmärchen*, or literary fantasy, that has constituted one of the major genres of German literature for the past two centuries. In 1900, when he was finding his way as a writer and experimenting with the various forms offered by the German romantic tradition, Hesse was inspired principally by E. T. A. Hoffmann, whom he regarded as the "Romantic storyteller of the greatest virtuosity." "Lulu," an autonomous section of the early novel entitled *The Posthumous Writings and Poems of Hermann Lauscher* (1901), is based explicitly and in specific detail on Hoffmann's classic fantasy *The Golden Flower Pot* (1813). The tale was inspired by a holiday trip that Hesse made in August of 1899 with a group of friends from Tübingen who called themselves (as in the story) the *petit cénacle* and whose names and sobriquets are playfully modified in the text. By means of the Hoffmannesque device of an encapsulated myth, Hesse succeeds in narrating the story of their collective infatuation with the innkeeper's niece (named in reality Julie Hellmann) in such a manner that it occurs on two levels: a "realistic" one as well as a fantastic or higher one. Through his skillful and ironic imitation of the romantic conventions Hesse paid his greatest tribute to Hoffmann.

Soon Hesse rejected the neoromanticism of his youth and turned to a less fanciful type of narrative after the fashion of the great nineteenth-century realists. To be sure, the impulse toward fantasy was not simply to be denied. In "Hannes," Hesse offered a realistic depiction of a contemporary who—because his consciousness has not yet undergone the characteristically modern dissociation and who therefore still enjoys a *Märchen* mentality that enables him to see God in the thunderclouds and to encounter Jesus on remote rural paths—is regarded by his neighbors as a simpleton. In general, however, having to find other outlets for his fantasy, Hesse chose a form consistent with his current realism—the legend, a genre in which the supernatural was not entirely implausible because it could be attributed to the mythic consciousness that existed in remote times and places (patristic Gaza in "The Enamored Youth," Renaissance Italy in "The Merman," seventeenth-century Berlin in "Three Lindens," and prehistoric jungles in "The Man of the Forests"). As we noted, however, the supernatural occurrences in the legends are regarded as an interruption of normal "reality" and not, as in the fairy

(xvii

tales, as self-evident. But Hesse soon found other ways of dealing with fantasy.

Dreams always played a lively role in Hesse's psychic life, as he tells us in the late essay "Nocturnal Games." The ominous precognitive dream of war related in "The Dream of the Gods" (1914) is significant because it signaled the unleashing of the powers of fantasy that Hesse had sought for more than a decade to suppress. During World War I, a variety of pressures—the death of his father, the deteriorating mental health of his first wife, the responsibilities for his three young sons, the burdens of his war-relief work in Switzerland—produced in Hesse an emotional crisis so severe that, in 1916 and 1917, he sought help in psychoanalysis. It was Jungian analysis, with its emphasis on dreams and their interpretation, that enabled Hesse to recover the childlike contact with the world of fantasy that he had attempted so long to repress. Hesse recognized what he owed to the insights of depth psychology. In a review of Oskar A. Schmitz's *Fairy Tales from the Unconscious* (*Märchen aus dem Unbewußten*, 1933), Hesse observed: "Finally, with the aid of a psychoanalytical method, he overcame the inhibitions that cut him off from his own fantasy and wrote these very readable fairy tales." Hesse is speaking from personal experience because several of the fairy tales that he wrote during the war are barely disguised metaphors for the recovery of the past through psychoanalysis: notably, "Iris" and "The Hard Passage." And in many of his fictional works—e.g., *Demian* and *Steppenwolf*—dreams function as an outlet for fantasy.

Introduction

Hesse was fully aware of the significance of the wartime *Märchen* and dreams in his personal development. In August of 1919 he wrote his publisher that *Demian* along with the *Märchen* that he composed from 1913 to 1918 were "tentative efforts toward a liberation, which I now regard as virtually complete." By means of the fairy tale, he had succeeded in reestablishing the link with the unconscious that had been ruptured. Yet the fairy tale as a genre was only a passing phase in his literary career. In another letter of August 1919, he wrote to a friend that "the *Märchen* were for me the transition to a new and different kind of writing; I no longer even like them." This wholesale rejection of his *Märchen* was a bit premature; some of his most charming efforts in the genre were still to come. However, the tone begins to change from the high seriousness of the wartime fables to the irony of "The Painter" and "Tale of the Wicker Chair," which anticipate Hesse's movement toward social satire in the twenties.

It is no accident that these two fantasies deal with painters, for toward the end of the war years Hesse had discovered in painting a new avocation. For a time, indeed, he toyed with the notion of attempting an entirely new career as an artist rather than a writer. Although this shift did not come about, Hesse continued to paint until the end of his life. (Indeed, his accomplishments as a painter have only recently come to be more widely appreciated, thanks to major exhibits of his work since the centenary of his birth in 1977). For many years, moreover, he earned money for special purposes—during World War I for his

war-relief work, and then during the thirties for the relief
of refugees from Nazi Germany—by producing holograph
editions of his poems on commission: characteristically, a
handwritten copy of a poem, or group of poems, accompanied by original watercolor illustrations. "Pictor's Metamorphoses" (*pictor* is the Latin word for "painter")
celebrates and exemplifies this activity.

Following the separation from his first wife in 1919,
Hesse moved to southern Switzerland, where he at first
lived a relatively isolated life. Coming to realize eventually
that this solitude was neither natural to him nor productive, the mid-fortyish writer courted and, in 1924, was
briefly married to a much younger woman, the singer Ruth
Wenger. "Pictor's Metamorphoses" amounts to an allegorical account, in fantasy form, of that love affair. The
painter, entering the paradise of Ticino (as depicted in the
accompanying aquarelles), first lives alone as a tree and
then, recognizing his mistake, reenters the natural cycle of
transformations by attaching himself to a beautiful young
woman. It is significant that, apart from a limited edition
in 1925, Hesse did not allow this work to be published until
a facsimile edition of an early version was brought out in
1954. Here the text is so closely tied to the watercolor
illustrations—indeed, the text emerges from them, as
Hesse wrote to Romain Rolland when he sent a presentation copy—that the full meaning is apparent only when
word and image are taken together. For three decades Hesse
took enormous satisfaction from preparing new holographs
of this fairy tale, in which the impulse toward fantasy is as

pronounced in the illustrations as in the story itself. (The illustrations reproduced in this volume are those that Hesse did for a copy he presented in 1923 to Ruth Wenger.)

Hesse was by no means the only writer of his generation to be attracted to the genre of fairy tale or fantasy. Indeed, no period since German romanticism produced as many fairy tales as the years around World War I. This fact was noted by early reviewers of Hesse's first published volume of *Märchen* (1919). One reviewer, observing that so many new editions of old fairy-tale collections had appeared since the turn of the century and that so many writers had tried their hand at the form, concluded that "in certain epochs a particular preference for *Märchen* makes itself felt, not only on the part of the creators, but also on the part of the recipients. For, in the life of the spirit, supply and demand often reflect each other." The benefit of hindsight has prompted literary scholars to inquire if perhaps a hidden affinity exists between the forms and contextual potentialities of the fairy tale and the ideas and goals of German expressionism. For virtually every major writer associated with expressionism experimented with the genre, including Hugo Ball, Ernst Barlach, Bertolt Brecht, Alfred Döblin, and Kurt Schwitters.

While a fascination with the unconscious world of dreams is conspicuous in expressionism, students of the period have emphasized in particular the socio-critical purposes to which the fairy tale was often devoted. The next group of Hesse's fantasies is certainly consistent with that generational tendency (notably, "The Tourist City in the

South," "Among the Massagetae," "King Yu," and "Bird").
The techniques of the fantasy—reification of abstract concepts within the framework of a simplified moral system—lend themselves to the exposure of existing social and cultural ills. Hesse shared the expressionist sense that the old social order was collapsing and that a new humanity was going to emerge from that chaos. So Hesse's use of the *Märchen* reflected the literary trends of the times, a fact of literary history that should be kept in mind if we hope to evaluate these works properly.

Hesse's late stories, while they bring no new variations in form, nevertheless display his continuing experimentation with the forms of fantasy. Indeed, the narrative is often encapsulated within a speculative framework in which the writer reflects on the nature of fantasy. "Nocturnal Games" embeds the account of several dreams in a rumination on the meaning of dreams in Hesse's life. "Report from Normalia," the fragment of an unfinished novel that might well have grown into a satirical counterpart to the utopian vision of *The Glass Bead Game*, depicts a Central European country "in the north of Aquitaine." "Normalia," we are told, emerged by expansion from the parklike grounds of a onetime insane asylum to become the most rational nation in Europe. But Hesse, making use of a fictional device that has recently appealed to writers of the absurd, casts doubt on all our assumptions concerning "normality." The narrator, it turns out, is ultimately unsure whether the former madhouse he inhabits has indeed become the seat of sanity in a mad world or whether it is not in fact still a madhouse. In "Christmas with Two Children's Stories" the two fairy tales—Hesse's own and the tale written by his grandson—generate a theoretical digression on the function and nature of fantasy. And in "The Jackdaw"—another example of Hesse's recurrent identification with birds—Hesse shares with us the manner in which his imagination plays with reality to generate stories about an unusually tame bird that he encounters at the spa in Baden. "And yet our imagination is not always satisfied with the most plausible explanation, it also likes to play with the remote and the sensational, and so I have conceived of two further possibilities beyond the probable one."

While fantasy in the unadulterated form that it displays in "Pictor's Metamorphoses" (where we are dealing literally with an "other-world" in Tolkien's sense) occurs infrequently in Hesse's mature works, it is fair to say that the tendency toward fantasy is evident in his writing from childhood to old age. Indeed, fantasy can be called the hallmark of Hesse's major novels of the twenties and thirties, the surreal quality that disturbs critics of a more realistic persuasion: for instance, the Magic Theater in *Steppenwolf* or the fanciful scenes in *The Journey to the East*, where reality blends into myth and fantasy. Indeed, fantasy is a state of mind into which Hesse and his literary surrogates enter with remarkable ease. Toward the end of *Demian*, for instance, Emil Sinclair encounters his friend after a long separation and is introduced into the enchanted home presided over by Demian's mysterious mother. Once again, we find the familiar juxtaposition of reality and fantasy. "Outside was reality: streets and houses, people and institutions, libraries and lecture halls —but here inside was love; here lived fantasy [*das Märchen*] and the dream." And what, after all, is the province of Castalia as depicted in Hesse's last great novel, *The Glass Bead Game*, if not a magnificent and sustained projection of a fantasy? In sum: any complete appreciation of Hesse must take into account this central tendency in his work. The most concentrated period of *Märchen* composition occurred, as noted, from 1913 to 1918, and the eight fantasies of those years were published in 1919 in a volume with the simple generic title *Märchen* (translated as *Strange News from Another Star and Other Tales*). However, the sustained obsession with fantasy in its various manifestations—folktale, literary fairy tale, dream, satire, rumination—is apparent only in a collection like the present one, which contains nineteen fantasies in chronological sequence covering a period of more than sixty years.

It would be a mistake to regard the tendency toward fantasy, in Hesse or other writers, as mere escapism. True, the classic periods of fantasy have been those ages (Napoleonic Germany, Victorian England, Weimar Germany, and America in the 1960s) when technological reality was perceived as so overwhelming that the individual began to question its values and measure them against other ideals. But fantasy, with its explicitly didactic tendency, represents not so much a flight from confrontation as, rather, a mode in which the confrontation can be enacted in a realm of esthetic detachment, where clear ethical judgments are possible. Indeed, fantasy often reveals the values of a given epoch more vividly than the so-called realisms it may bring forth. In any case, a generation that decorates its walls with the calendars of the Brothers Hildebrandt while perusing Tolkien's *Lord of the Rings*, that hastens from meetings of the C. S. Lewis Society to performances of space fantasies like *Star Wars*, has mastered the semiotics necessary to decode the hidden signs of "Pictor's Metamorphoses" and Hesse's other fantasies.

THEODORE ZIOLKOWSKI

PICTOR'S
METAMORPHOSES
AND OTHER FANTASIES

Lulu

A YOUTHFUL ESCAPADE

In Memory of E. T. A. Hoffmann

I

THE LOVELY OLD TOWN of Kirchheim had just been washed clean by a brief summer downpour. Everything looked new and fine; the red rooftops, the weather vanes and garden fences, the shrubs and chestnut trees along the embankments shimmered gaily in the sun, and the statue of Konrad Widerhold with his stony better half, agleam in the quiet light, enjoyed its robust old age. The warm sun shone through the purified air with renewed strength, turning the last raindrops that hung on the branches into blazing sparks; the inviting, broad path along the embankment was flooded with splendor. Children skipped happily along in a row, a little dog yelped exultantly at their heels; along the line of houses, a yellow butterfly traced restless curves in flight.

Under the embankment's chestnut trees, on the third bench to the right of the post office, beside his friend Ludwig Ugel, sat the itinerant aesthete Hermann Lauscher, who launched a spirited and charming discourse on the benefactions of the newly fallen rain and the reemergence of the azure of the heavens, embellishing his monologue with fanciful observations about matters which were close to his heart, tirelessly rambling, as was his wont, on the meadow of his rhetoric. During the course of the poet's long, eloquent address, the amused and silent Herr Ludwig Ugel repeatedly cast sharp glances toward the main road to Boihingen, looking out for a friend who would be coming to meet them.

"Don't you agree?" the poet cried out with gusto as he rose up slightly from the bench. Its straight back had become uncomfortable. What's more, Lauscher had been sitting on some dry twigs. "Isn't it just as I say?" he repeated, while his left hand brushed away the twigs and smoothed out the creases they had made in his trousers. "The Essence of Beauty must lie in Light! Don't you agree that that's where it is?"

Ludwig Ugel rubbed his eyes; he had not been listening to what his friend was saying and had only caught Lauscher's last question.

"Certainly, certainly," he hastily replied. "But from here you can hardly see a thing. It's just over there, in back of the Schlotterbecks' barn!"

"What? What did you say?" Lauscher demanded vehemently. "What's in back of the barn?"

"Why, Oetlingen, of course! Karl's got to be coming from there; there isn't any other way."

Disagreeable and silent now too, the itinerant poet fixed his eyes on the bright, broad main road. And we can leave these two young men sitting and waiting on their bench; the shade is sure to last there for another hour. In the meantime, let us turn our attention beyond the Schlotter-becks' barn. There we will find neither the village of Oetlingen nor the Essence of Beauty, but rather the awaited third friend, the student of jurisprudence Karl Hamelt, returning from Wendlingen, where he had spent his vacation.

Though not misshapen, his figure, in growing prematurely plump, had acquired a touch of the comical in its corpulence; in his shrewd and capricious face, a powerful nose and oddly plump lips were at odds with inordinately full cheeks. His broad chin fell in rich fleshy folds over his narrow stand-up collar; and his short hair, in disarray and sopping with perspiration, brazenly stuck out between his hat and his forehead. Stretched out to full length on his back in the grass, he gave every appearance of sleeping peacefully.

Tired from traveling in the midday heat, he really had fallen asleep; but his slumber was far from peaceful. A most singular and fantastic dream troubled it. He dreamed that he lay in an unfamiliar garden, under strange trees, reading an old book whose pages were of parchment. The book was written in characters that boldly and chaotically looped and tangled through one another, in a completely foreign language, one which Hamelt neither recognized nor understood. And yet he could read and understand the contents of the pages; for again and again—whenever he grew tired—out of the inextricable tangle of flourishes and script, pictures magically arose, shone in bright colors, and again sank out of sight. These pictures, flashing up one after another as in a magic lantern, portrayed the following, extremely old, true story.

THAT SAME DAY on which the talisman of the bronze ring was stolen from the Laskian Spring by means of black magic and fell into the hands of the Prince of Dwarfs, the bright star of the House of Ask began to pale. The Laskian Spring dried up into naught but a barely visible silver thread. The earth beneath the Opal Palace began to sink; the subterranean vaults swayed and started to crack. Great devastation befell the lily garden; the double-crowned royal lily alone managed to hold itself proud and tall, but only for a little while, for the Serpent Edelzung had breathed a tight lasso of hoarfrost around its stem. In the desolate City of Ask, all gaiety and music were silenced; since the last string of the Harp Silversong had snapped, not a note of music sounded even in the Opal Palace. Day and night the King sat by himself, like a statue, in the great banquet hall; he could not cease marveling at the decline of his happiness, for he had been the happiest of all kings since Mirthful the Great. A sad sight he was to behold, King Sorrowless in his red robes, sitting in his great hall, marveling and marveling; he could not weep, he had been born without the gift of sorrow. And he marveled at still another thing: mornings and evenings, instead of the music he was accustomed to hearing played, there was only a huge silence, and from behind the door to her room, the gentle weeping of Princess Lilia. Only rarely did a brief, austere burst of laughter shake the King's broad chest, and this merely out of habit. In former times, not a blessed day had passed without his laughing twice four-and-twenty times.

His retinue and servants had scattered to the four winds; apart from the King in the hall and the sorrowing Princess Lilia, only one member of the household remained: the faithful servant Haderbart, who, besides filling the posts of court poet and court philosopher, performed the duties of court jester as well.

But now the Prince of Dwarfs shared the power of the bronze talisman with the Witch Poisonbreath, and one can imagine to what ends they used it.

The glorious days of the House of Ask were coming to an end. On the evening of a day on which the King had not laughed even once, he summoned the Princess Lilia and the faithful Haderbart into his presence in the empty banquet hall. A thunderstorm filled the sky; framed by the huge, black, vaulted windows, sudden bolts of lightning palely lit the hall.

"I haven't laughed at all today, not even once," said King Sorrowless.

The court jester stood before the King and pulled one of his most audacious faces; but the grimace made his troubled old face look so distorted and desperate that the Princess had to avert her eyes, and the King just shook his heavy head without laughing.

"Music! Bring out the Harp Silversong!" King Sorrowless commanded. "Music, there must be music!" he said, and his cry sorrowfully resounded in the hearts of the other two; for the King did not know that the harpist and all the other musicians had left him, these two faithful companions being all that remained of his household.

"The Harp Silversong no longer has any strings," said the faithful Haderbart.

"No matter, it must be played," said the King.

Then Haderbart took Princess Lilia by the hand and left the hall. Through the withered lily garden he led her up to the dried out Laskian Spring, scooped up the last handful of water from its marble basin, and poured it into her right hand; then they returned into the presence of the King. From the Laskian water the Princess fashioned seven shining silver strings for the Harp Silversong; but there was not enough water for the eighth, and she had to make it with the help of her own tears. And now, her empty, trembling hand gently stroked the strings of the harp, so that once again the old, sweet, joyful sound issued and swelled blissfully. But no sooner had she plucked a string than it snapped, and when the last string sounded and broke, an enormous thunderbolt burst from the heavens, and the whole vault of the Opal Palace came crashing down. But the last Song of the Harp went as follows:

> *Hushed Silversong will be,*
> *Both harp and melody,*
> *But on its strings will sound someday*
> *Once more this ancient roundelay.*

(End of the true story of the Laskian waters.)

Lulu

THE STUDENT Karl Hamelt did not awaken from his dream before his two friends—having grown impatient—had walked down the road a bit and found him lying in the grass. They reproached him in no uncertain terms for his dawdling. Hamelt responded with silence, except for bidding them "Good morning" with a cursory nod. This made Ugel especially indignant. "Good morning, indeed!" he flared. "It hasn't been morning for some time! Couldn't wait for us, eh? I can see you've been to the tavern in Oetlingen; the wine's still glowing in your eyes!"

Karl sneered and pulled his brown felt hat farther down over his brow. "Never mind," said Lauscher. The three friends turned toward the town, passed the railroad station, crossed the bridge over the stream, then meandered along the embankment until they reached the King's Crown. Not only was this inn their favorite Kirchheim watering hole, it was also the temporary lodgings of the itinerant poet.

As the three friends approached the stairs that led to the inn, the heavy doors of the house suddenly flew open, and plummeting toward them at lightning speed came a highly agitated, white-haired man with a gray beard and an angry red face. In consternation, the friends recognized the old crank and philosopher Turnabout, and they barred his way at the foot of the stairs.

"Stop right there, my good Herr Turnabout!" the poet Lauscher called out to him. "How does it happen that a philosopher can lose his sense of balance like this? Just turn around, my esteemed fellow, and tell us your troubles inside, where it's cool!"

(9

With a sidelong, acute look of distrust, the philosopher raised his shaggy head and peered at the three young men. "Oh, so it's you," he cried. "The whole petit cénacle! You'd better hurry and go inside, my friends. Go in and drink your beer and wonder at what you'll find in there; but please don't insist on the company of this poor, broken-down old man, whose heart and brain are in the clutches of demons!"

"But, dear Herr Turnabout, whatever is the matter with you today?" Ludwig Ugel asked sympathetically. But immediately thereafter he found himself staggering from the blow of the philosopher's fist in his side, and propped himself up against the railing of the staircase. The old man ran down the street, cursing and raging.

"Infamous Poisonbreath," he bellowed as he hurried off, "ill-fated talisman, transformed into a red-blue flower! Abused, trampled in the dust, the only . . . Victim of satanical malice . . . The excruciating memory revived . . ."

The three friends shook their heads in astonishment and let the rampaging man go his way. At long last they began to ascend the stairs, when once again the doors flew open, and, with a friendly gesture of adieu to those still inside, Parson Wilhelm Wingolf stepped out. Those who stood on the stairs greeted him with all good cheer, and immediately inquired as to the cause of the radiance that gilded his broad and most worthy head. Mysteriously, he raised his chubby index finger, took the poet confidentially aside, and with a roguish smile whispered into his ear, "Just think, today, for the first time in my life, I have made a verse! And I did it not a moment ago!"

The poet opened his eyes so wide that they circled above and below the narrow frames of his wire-rimmed spectacles. "Recite it!" he cried. The parson turned toward the three friends, again raised his finger, and with blissfully half-closed eyes he recited his verse:

> *Perfection,*
> *Today you've peered in my direction!*

And, without uttering another word, he took his leave of the comrades, waving his hat.

"Good God!" said Ludwig Ugel. The poet stood silent, lost in thought. But Karl Hamelt, who had not let a single word pass his lips since he'd awakened in the grass, emphatically announced, "What a good poem!"

At this point, expecting the unexpected, the thirsty friends finally managed, without further hindrance, to enter the cool parlor of the Crown. It was much the best room, for in it the young wife of the innkeeper waited on the customers herself; furthermore, at this time of day they could count on being the only guests and could practice their jocular good manners on their hostess.

The first remarkable thing that all three noticed as soon as they entered and took their seats was this: today, for the very first time, the small, round hostess no longer seemed at all pretty. This, however, was owing to something each of them quickly remarked to himself in silence.

Towering above the polished ornate border of the roomy sideboard, in semi-darkness, was the head of a strange and beautiful young maiden.

2

THE SECOND, no less remarkable thing was that the elegant Herr Erich Tänzer—one of the inner circle of the cénacle and the bosom friend of Karl Hamelt—though seated at the small table immediately beside that of his friends, in no way remarked or acknowledged their arrival. Before him on the table was a half-full glass of light beer, into which he had placed a yellow rose. He sat there slowly rolling his big, somewhat bulging eyes; and for the first time in his life he looked utterly ridiculous. From time to time he lowered his stately nose closer to the flower and sniffed at it, while simultaneously casting a nearly impossible sidelong glance at the unknown woman's face. Despite the complete transformation of his own visage, hers showed not the slightest change of expression.

And the third extraordinary thing was that Turnabout, quite calm and composed, was sitting next to Erich. In the old man's glass, a few drops of Kulmbacher remained; stuck in his mouth was one of the Crown's Cuban cigars.

"What the devil, Herr Turnabout!" Hermann Lauscher exclaimed as he leaped to his feet. "How ever did you get in here? Didn't I just see you run off toward the upper embankment?"

"And didn't you, not a moment ago, in the fiercest rage, plant your fist in my stomach?" cried Ludwig Ugel.

"No harm intended," replied the philosopher, his most winning smile on his lips. "Please don't take it amiss, dear Herr Ugel! My good sirs, let me recommend the Kulmbacher!" So saying, he calmly drained his glass.

Meanwhile, Karl Hamelt called out to his friend Erich, who still sat dreamily entranced before the yellow rose in his beer glass. "Erich, are you asleep?"

Without looking up, Erich answered, "I are not asleep."

"You can't say 'I *are* asleep.' You say, 'I *am* asleep!'" cried Ugel.

But just then, the girl's head moved from behind the sideboard, and a moment later her whole, lovely, unfamiliar person stood at the friends' table. "What would the gentlemen like?"

He who has never stood entranced before a woman's portrait and suddenly beheld the beauty come to life, stepping forth from the painted landscape, cannot possibly imagine what the cénacle brothers felt at this moment. All three rose from their chairs and made three deep bows, one each.

"Lovely, beloved lady!" said the poet. "Most gracious Fräulein!" said Ludwig Ugel. Karl Hamelt was speechless.

"Is it Kulmbacher you're drinking?" the beauty asked.

"Yes, please," said Ludwig; Karl nodded in assent; Lauscher, though, ordered a glass of red wine.

While the girl's slender hands elegantly served the

(13

drinks, another round of self-conscious, deferential compliments was paid. Then Frau Müller came running from her corner of the room.

"Don't make such a lot of fuss, gentlemen, over this silly girl," she said. "She's my stepsister and has come here to work because we were shorthanded . . . Go into the buffet, Lulu; it's not proper for a young lady to dawdle about with the men."

Lulu slowly walked away. The philosopher furiously champed down on his cigar; Erich Tänzer cast another acrobatic glance toward where the girl had vanished. The three friends, irritated and embarrassed, fell silent.

To appear to be friendly and to make conversation, the hostess took a flowerpot from the windowsill and brought it over to the men's table, making a proud display of it. "Just look at this extraordinary flower! It may well be the rarest known to man, and they say that it blooms but once every five or ten years."

All eyes turned toward the red-blue flower nodding gently on its long, bare stem, emitting a strangely musty scent. The philosopher became greatly agitated and cast a fiercely cutting glance at the hostess and her flower; but no one noticed this.

Quite suddenly, Erich sprang to his feet, dashed over to his friends' table, forcibly seized and tore the flower in two, and with its two halves disappeared into the buffet. Turnabout burst out in a fit of malicious laughter. The hostess let out an ear-piercing shriek and set off after Tänzer, but she caught her dress on a chair and went tumbling to the floor. Ugel, in hot pursuit, stumbled over her, and over him the poet, who, in leaping to his feet, sent both wine goblet and flowerpot crashing to the floor. The philosopher fell upon the helplessly prostrate hostess, shook his fists in her face, bared his teeth, completely oblivious of Ugel and Lauscher, who struggled madly to pull him off by tearing at his coattails. At this moment the innkeeper ran in; the philosopher, as if transformed, helped the woman to her feet. In the doorway of the adjacent room, farmers and carters stood gaping at the scandalous scene. The lovely Lulu could be heard weeping in the buffet, out of which Erich emerged, crumpled flower in hand. Everyone rushed upon him and set to scolding, questioning, threatening, ridiculing him; but he, brandishing the broken flower, desperately cut through the crowd, and, without his hat, attained the outdoors.

3

THE NEXT MORNING, Karl Hamelt, Erich Tänzer, and Ludwig Ugel gathered in Hermann Lauscher's room at the inn to hear him read his latest poems. Everyone served himself from a big carafe of wine standing on the table. The poet had already recited several charming poems, and now he extracted the last one, written on a small piece of paper, from his breast pocket. He began: "To the Princess Lilia . . ."

"What?" cried Karl Hamelt, rising up from the settee. Somewhat annoyed, Lauscher repeated the title. But Karl,

now deep in thought, settled back on the flowery cushions.
The poet read:

I know an ancient roundelay,
O clear, bright Silversong!
How softly you are ringing,
Like fiddle bows across heartstrings,
Music that sounds of home . . .

Hamelt completely distracted the others' attention from
the rest of the song. "Princess Lilia . . . Silversong . . . the
ancient roundelay . . ." he said over and over again, shaking his head. Then he rubbed his forehead, stared blankly
into the air, and fixed his glowing, intense gaze on the poet.
When Lauscher finished reading, he looked up to meet
this gaze. "What is it?" he asked astonished. "Are you
practicing your rattlesnake eye on me, a poor defenseless
bird?"

Hamelt awakened, as if from a deep dream. "Where did
that song come from?" he asked the poet in a soft voice.
Lauscher shrugged. "Where they all come from," he replied.

"And Princess Lilia?" Hamelt asked on. "And the ancient
roundelay? Don't you see that this is the only real song you
have ever composed? All your other poems . . ."

Lauscher was quick to interrupt him. "All right, that's
enough; but in fact," he went on, "in point of fact, my dear
friend, the song is an enigma to me, too. I was just sitting
around, my mind a complete blank, when, out of habit and
to pass the time, I started scribbling on a piece of paper—

doodling, and drawing decorative letters; when I stopped, there on the paper was the song. It's in a completely different handwriting from the one in which I generally write; see for yourselves!"

He gave the paper to Erich, who was sitting beside him. Erich held it up to his eyes and could hardly believe what he saw. He looked at it a second time, more closely, then sank back into his chair, exclaiming loudly, "Lulu!" Ugel and Hamelt rushed over to have a look at the paper. "Good heavens!" Ugel exclaimed. Hamelt, however, sank back on the settee, eyeing the extraordinary page and exhibiting every sign of utter astonishment. Supreme joy and profound gloom alternately passed over his features.

"Now tell me, Lauscher," he said at last, "is this our Lulu, or is it the Princess Lilia?"

"What tripe!" the poet cried in anger. "Give it back to me!"

But while he held the page in his hand and looked at it once again, quite suddenly a strange, cold terror came over him, making his heart skip a beat. The erratic, mutable letters mysteriously ran together to form the contours of a head. As Lauscher continued to pore over the page, the fine features of a girl's face emerged, in the likeness of none other than the strange and beautiful Lulu.

Erich sat, as if turned to stone, in his chair; Karl lay mumbling on the settee; beside him sat Ludwig Ugel, who could do nothing but shake his head. The poet stood in the middle of the room, pale and lost. Then a hand tapped him on the shoulder; frightened, he turned around to find the philosopher Turnabout, who doffed his shabby, pointed hat in greeting.

"Turnabout!" the poet exclaimed in astonishment. "My God, did you fall through the ceiling?"

"What do you mean, Herr Lauscher?" replied the smiling old man. "Whatever do you mean? I knocked twice. But let me see what you've got there. Aha, a splendid manuscript." He took the song, or rather the picture, carefully from Lauscher's hands. "You'll permit me to examine it, won't you? Since when did you start collecting rare manuscripts?"

"Rare manuscripts? Collecting? So you think you'll learn something from that scrap of paper?" The old man continued to examine and finger the page with great delight.

"Well, really," he said with a grin, "it is a lovely fragment of a text, even if corrupt, and late. It's Askian."

"Askian?" Hamelt called out.

"No doubt about it, Herr Student," the philosopher replied in a friendly tone. "But tell me now, my dear Herr Lauscher, tell me where you came upon this exceedingly rare find. Further investigations are in order!"

"Come, come now, Herr Turnabout, stop telling tales," the poet rejoined with a nervous laugh. "It's brand-new, I penned it myself last night."

The philosopher measured up Lauscher with a suspicious look. "I must confess," he replied, "I really must confess, my fine young man, that I have a strong distaste for this sort of tomfoolery."

Lulu

Lauscher became earnestly indignant. "Herr Turnabout," he cried vehemently, "I must beseech you not to take me for a buffoon, and in the event that you yourself, as it appears, would like to play that merry role, kindly select some theater other than my lodgings for your performance."

"Now, now." Turnabout smiled good-naturedly. "Maybe you'd like to give the matter some more thought! Meanwhile, farewell, fare you all well, my good sirs!" So saying, he righted his shimmering green cap on his head of white hair and quietly left the room.

Downstairs, in the empty tavern, Turnabout found the lovely Lulu standing alone, drying wineglasses with a towel. He went over to the keg and helped himself to a mug of beer; then he sat down at the table opposite the girl. He did not try to make conversation, but from time to time his friendly, old, bright eyes looked into the beauty's face; and she, sensing his kindly intentions, went calmly about her work. The philosopher then took one of the empty cut-glass goblets, poured in some water, moistened the glass's rim, and began to run the tip of his index finger around it. Soon a humming arose, then a clear ringing tone, which alternately swelled and diminished, filling the whole room with its sound. The lovely Lulu enjoyed the glass's singing; her hands stopped what they were doing, and she listened, completely captivated by the eternally sweet, crystal-clear tones. From time to time, the old man looked up from the glass and into her eyes, amiably and searchingly. The whole room rang with the singing of the glass. Lulu stood calmly in the middle of the room, her mind a blank; she listened intently, her eyes growing wide as a child's.

"Is the old King Sorrowless still alive?" she heard a voice ask, not knowing if it came from the old man or from the singing glass. Not knowing why, she had to nod in assent.

"And do you still remember the Song of the Harp Silversong?"

She had to nod and did not know why. The crystal tones rang even more softly. The voice asked: "Where are the strings of the Harp Silversong?"

The tone grew fainter still and died away in delicate, shallow waves. And then, not knowing the reason, the lovely Lulu began to weep.

A hush fell over the room, and so it remained for some time.

"Why are you weeping, Lulu?" Turnabout asked.

"Oh, have I been weeping?" she shyly answered. "I was trying to remember a song from my childhood; but I could only recall half of it."

Suddenly the door flew open and Frau Müller burst in. "What's going on here? Still on those same glasses?" she scolded. Lulu began to cry again, the hostess went on grumbling and grouching at her; neither of them noticed the philosopher—who was smoking a short-stemmed pipe —blow a huge ring of smoke, enter into its midst, and, on a gentle draft of air, imperceptibly vanish through the open window.

4

THE MEMBERS of the petit cénacle had gathered in the neighboring woods. Even the junior barrister Oscar Ripplein had joined them there. A great many enthusiastic words about youth and friendship issued from the mouths of the comrades, who lay on the grass; and their discussion was interrupted as often by laughter as by contemplative pauses. Most of the talk centered on the poet's thoughts and opinions; for the next day he would set off on a journey, and none of them knew when or if they would see him again.

"I must go abroad," said Hermann Lauscher. "I need to go off by myself and once again breathe fresh air. Perhaps one day I'll be only too happy to return; but, for the time being, I've had about all I can take of the narrow confines of student life; I'm sick to death of the abominable groves of belle academe. Everything seems to stink of beer and tobacco; besides, these last few years I've absorbed more knowledge than is good for a poet."

"Do you hear what you're saying?" Oscar broke in. "I thought we had enough uneducated artists, particularly poets."

"Perhaps," Lauscher retorted. "But education and knowledge are two very different things. What I had in mind was the danger of gradually studying yourself into that damned state of self-consciousness. Everything must go through the brain, everything must be grasped and measured. You put things to the test; you measure yourself, seeking out the limits of your talents; you become your own experimental subject, and finally you see—too late—that you've left the better part of your self and your art far behind you, in the oft-ridiculed, subconscious impulses and emotions of early youth. Now you are reaching out to embrace the sunken Isle of Innocence; but you no longer do so at the wholehearted and heedless prompting of sorrow deeply felt. No—even this gesture is self-conscious, premeditated, a pose."

"What's really on your mind?" Karl Hamelt asked, with a smile.

"You already know," cried Hermann. "Yes, I'll admit that the book I recently published troubles me. I must learn anew how to create out of the plenum, to go back to where all things begin. It's not so much that I want to write something 'new.' What I need is new experiences, a fresh, clean, healthy strip of life to live. I want, as in my childhood, to lie down on the banks of streams, to climb mountains, to play my fiddle, to run after girls, to take whatever life—whatever each day—has to offer; I want to wait for my poems to come to me, instead of breathlessly and anxiously hunting them down."

"Right you are," the voice of Turnabout suddenly chimed in. He had emerged from the woods and stood in the midst of the young men's camp.

"Turnabout!" they all exclaimed merrily. "Good day, Herr Philosopher! Good morning, Herr Ubiquitous!"

The old man sat down, took a deep drag on his cigar, and turned his well-meaning, friendly face toward the poet

Lauscher. "There's still a young man inside me," he began with a smile, "who would very much enjoy having a good long talk with the likes of you. If you'll permit me, I'd like to join your discussion."

"With pleasure," said Karl Hamelt. "Our friend Lauscher was just saying that a poet has to return to the wellsprings of the unconscious, knowledge and learning being of little use to him."

"Rather nicely put," the old man replied slowly. "I've always felt a certain kinship with poets and have gotten to know quite a few on whom my friendship was not entirely wasted. Poets, even today, more so than other people, are inclined to believe in certain stable, eternal forces and concepts of Beauty which lie half-asleep in the womb of life. The intimation of which sometimes shines through the enigmatic present as summer lightning shines through the night. In such moments of illumination, it seems to them that all ordinary life and they with it are nothing more than pictures limned on a lovely curtain; and only behind this curtain does genuine, true life go on. The most supreme, the most eternal words of the great poets seem— even to me—but the babblings of a dreamer who, without knowing it, murmurs through heavy lips of the heights of the world beyond, heights he has only briefly glimpsed."

"Very beautiful," Oscar Ripplein interjected, "very eloquently put, Herr Turnabout, but neither old nor new enough. These visionary sermons were preached some hundred years ago by the Romantics, as they were called: they, too, dreamed of such things, and of summer lightning. In schools today, one hears this referred to as a disease—fortunately eradicated—that only afflicts poets. But it's been years since anyone's dreamed such dreams, or, if he has, he understands that his brain . . ."

"That will do!" Karl Hamelt interrupted. "More than a hundred years ago, there also existed such . . . such 'brains,' who also bored everyone to tears with their long, dreary discussions. And nowadays those dreamers and visionaries seem even more charming and splendid than those all-too-readily understandable sly dogs. Speaking of dreams, I had an exceptional one today."

"Let's hear it, then!" the old man entreated.

"Some other time."

"You don't want to tell it? Then perhaps we can guess," said Turnabout. Karl Hamelt laughed out loud.

"Now, let's give it a try!" Turnabout persisted. "Each one of us will ask a question, to which you must truthfully reply either yes or no. Even if we don't guess your dream, we'll have had fun trying."

Everyone agreed to play the game, and questions came flying from all sides. The best questions were always those asked by the philosopher. When his turn came again, he asked, after some deliberation, "Was there water in your dream?"

"Yes."

Because the question had been answered in the affirmative, the old man was entitled to another turn.

"Springwater?"

"Yes."

"Water from a magic fountain?"

"Yes."

"Was the water scooped out?"

"Yes."

"By a girl?"

"Yes."

"No!" shouted Turnabout. "Think again!"

"But it was!"

"So you say a girl scooped out the water?"

"Yes."

Turnabout shook his head furiously. "Impossible!" he reiterated. "Did the girl scoop the water out of the fountain with her own hands?"

"Oh, no!" Karl exclaimed in confusion. "It was the faithful servant Haderbart who put his hands into the water."

"Ah, now we've got you!" the others exulted. And then Karl told the whole story of his dream of the Laskian Spring, to which everyone listened amazed and deeply moved.

"Princess Lilia!" Lauscher exclaimed. "And Silversong? Why are these names so familiar to me?"

"Indeed," said the old man, "both those names are in the Askian manuscript you showed me yesterday."

"In my song!" the poet sighed.

"In the picture of the beautiful Lulu," whispered Karl and Erich.

Meantime, the philosopher had lit another cigar and puffed hard on it, until he was almost entirely enveloped in a cloud of blue tobacco smoke.

"You smoke like a chimney," said Oscar Ripplein, extricating himself from the cloud. "And what a stinking weed!"

"Genuine Mexican!" the old man replied from inside his cloud. Then he stopped puffing, and presently a gust of wind blew up from behind, carrying off the redolent cloud and Turnabout with it.

Karl and Hermann pursued the vanishing smoke cloud into the woods. "What garbage!" growled the junior barrister, suddenly aware of an unpleasant feeling that he had fallen into dubious company. Erich and Ludwig had already made themselves scarce, and in the golden clarity of the late afternoon they strolled back toward Kirchheim and the Crown.

Karl and Hermann overtook the last fluttering wisps of tobacco smoke deep in the woods, and stood silent and perplexed before a large beech tree. They were about to sit down on a patch of moss, to catch their breath, when the voice of Turnabout spoke out from behind a tree. "Don't sit there, gentlemen, it's still damp! Come join me over here!"

They found the old man sitting on a huge, withered bough that sprawled on the ground like a shapeless dragon. "I'm glad you've come!" he said. "Please do take a seat near me! Your dream, Herr Hamelt, and your manuscript, Herr Lauscher, interest me."

"First," Hamelt stormed at him, "first, for heaven's sake, you must tell me how you managed to guess my dream!"

"And read my paper!" Lauscher added.

"Indeed!" said the old man. "What's to wonder about?

Lulu

You can guess anything if you ask the right questions. Besides, the story of Princess Lilia is so close to my heart it was only natural that I should recognize it."

"So that's it!" cried the student. "How do you happen to know this story, and how do you explain the sudden and conspicuous appearance of my dream—about which I had spoken to no one—in Lauscher's enigmatic song?"

The philosopher smiled and replied in a gentle voice: "When one has devoted oneself to the story of the Soul and its Salvation, as I have, one recognizes similar instances; they are innumerable. Of Princess Lilia's story there are many, highly divergent accounts. She wanders, displaced, like a ghost, through all the ages, taking on multiple guises, transforming herself; she particularly likes to manifest herself in the commodious form of the dream-vision. Only rarely does the Princess appear as herself, and only when the final stages of the purification process are near completion—only rarely, I say, does she take on human form, and she waits, unawares, for the moment of her salvation. I myself saw her not too long ago and attempted to talk to her. But she was as if in a dream, and when I ventured to ask her about the strings of the Harp Silversong, she burst into tears."

Wide-eyed, the young people listened to the philosopher. Admonitions and strange accords rose up in them; and yet Turnabout's oddly circuitous manner of speaking and his half-ironic facial expressions confused them, tying the threads of his story into one great Gordian knot.

"You, Herr Lauscher," he continued, "write on aesthetics

and must know how enticing and dangerous it is to span the narrow, but deep, cleft between the Good and the Beautiful. We need not despair that this cleft signifies an absolute separation, for we know, on the contrary, that the fissure betokens an essential Unity; that the Good and the Beautiful are not two distinct principles; rather, they are the daughters of the one principle: Truth. The two only appear as separate, hostile mountaintops—deep in the womb of the earth, they are one and the same. But what good does this insight do us, when we're left standing on one of these summits with the yawning abyss always before our eyes? The spanning of the abyss and the salvation of Princess Lilia are one. She is the blue flower, the sight of which disburdens the Soul, the scent of which distills all harshness, all obstinacy from the Spirit. She is the child who apportions kingdoms, the fruit of the combined longing of all the great souls. On the day she ripens and is saved, the Harp Silversong will sound, the Laskian Spring will rustle and rush through the restored, blossoming lily garden. And he who sees and perceives this, to him it will seem that his previous life was but one long nightmare, and now for the first time he would awaken to the clear light and the fresh sounds of a new day . . . But the Princess still languishes under the curse of the Witch Poisonbreath; the thunder of the evil hour still reverberates in the rubble-filled Opal Palace; and my King, shackled in leaden dream-chains, still lies in the devastated hall."

5

AN HOUR LATER, when the two friends came out of the woods, they caught sight of Ludwig Ugel, Erich Tänzer, and the junior barrister with a woman in a bright dress coming from the pub, strolling toward them up the mountain. With joy they recognized the slender Lulu and hastened toward the foursome with all due speed. She was cheerful and her gentle, loving voice sweetly mingled in their conversation. Halfway up the mountain, they sat down on a long bench. Below them, the town lay bright and cheerful in the valley; on all sides, the golden vapors of evening glistened on the high meadows. August munificently extended its dreamy fullness; in the trees' thick foliage, green fruits swelled; on the road in the valley, gleaming harvest wagons decorated with garlands made their way toward the villages and farmsteads.

"I don't know what makes these August evenings so beautiful," said Ludwig Ugel. "Still, they don't make you feel happy, they make you want to lie down in the high grass and become part of the gentle tenderness of the golden hour."

"Yes," Lauscher said, gazing into the pure, dark eyes of the beautiful Lulu. "Because the season is drawing to a close, we feel mellow and sad. How gently and wearily the ripe sweetness of summer spills over into these last days of August. And we know that tomorrow or the day after, somewhere or other, leaves will have already turned red and lie on the roads. In these hours you silently watch the slow turning of the Wheel of Time, and you feel yourself slowly and sadly being carried along with it . . . carried off somewhere . . . to that place where the red leaves lie."

They all fell silent, listening now to the sounds of the golden evening sky and the colorful landscape. Lulu began to hum very softly; gradually the melody went from a half-whisper to full-voiced singing.

The young men listened in silent rapture. The soft, sweet tones of her noble voice seemed to come from the very depths of the blessed evening, like dreams from the bosom of the slumbering earth.

> *From the clear expanse of sky,*
> *Peace and harmony gently fall;*
> *As do joy and suffering, all*
> *Like sweet songs, sweetly die.*

With this stanza the evening song was done. Then Ludwig Ugel, who lay on the grass at the feet of the others, began to sing:

> *O fountain in the forest, O Silverspring most clear,*
> *Down to the white chapel, through secret channels, steer!*
> *There on the mossy steps the Virgin Mary is.*
> *Call to her softly, murmur, tell her of my distress.*
> *Hush, speak gently, tell her, tell her of my need:*
> *My mouth is red with sin, and oh with singing red.*
> *Carry to her this lily, a pure white offering*
> *So that she may forgive me my red life and my sins.*
> *Perhaps her gracious smile will shine upon your face,*

Lulu

And from the pure white flower a sweet scent will arise:
Drinking in love and sunlight be all the singer's sins,
And only by her gracious kiss may Song's red mouth
    be cleansed.

And then Hermann Lauscher sang one of his songs:

> *The summer nods its weary head,*
> *Sees its pale image in the lake.*
> *Weary, dust-covered, still I tread*
> *The broad, shady road I must take.*
>
> *Weary, dust-covered, onward I tread;*
> *Behind me my youth stands still.*
> *Its shapely limbs, its lovely head*
> *Will not bend to my will.*

Meantime, the sun had set, suffusing the sky with red
hues. The overcautious junior barrister was about to remind everyone it was time to be getting home, when once
again the lovely Lulu began to sing:

> *Many a towering city,*
> *Many a stern fortress*
> *Stand in the realm of my father,*
> *The King called Sorrowless.*
>
> *And should a knight of valor*
> *Pledge troth and deliver me,*
> *To half my father's kingdom*
> *Heir he would rightly be.*

Now they all got up and slowly started back down the glowing mountain. On the other side of the summit of high Mount Teck, a late strip of sunlight gleamed and failed.

"Where did you learn that song?" Karl Hamelt asked the lovely Lulu.

"I really can't remember," she said. "I think it's a folksong." And she quickened her pace, suddenly seized by a fear of getting home too late and incurring the wrath of the innkeeper's wife.

"We won't let that happen," Erich Tänzer cried out. "In any event, I've been meaning to give Frau Müller a piece of my mind, to tell her exactly . . ."

"No, not that!" the lovely Lulu interrupted him. "Things will only get worse for me if you do! I'm just a poor orphan who must bear whatever burdens others place on me."

"Oh, Fräulein Lulu," said the barrister, "I wish you were a princess and that I could save you."

"No," cried the aesthete Lauscher, "you really are a princess. It's we who are not 'knight' enough to save you. But what's preventing us? I'll do it today. I'll take that damned Frau Müller by the throat . . ."

"Hush! Hush!" Lulu cried beseechingly. "Leave me to suffer my fate alone! I'm only sorry I'm not free to enjoy the rest of this lovely evening."

Little more was said as they quickly neared the town. There Lulu returned to the Crown alone; the others watched her disappear down a dark street.

Lulu

> *My father is the King,*
> *The King called Sorrowless* . . .

Karl Hamelt quietly hummed to himself as he made his way home to the village of Wendlingen.

6

LATER THAT SAME EVENING, Erich Tänzer bided his time in the Crown, waiting until Lauscher took his night light and went up to his room and he alone remained in the tavern. Alone, that is, with Lulu, who was still sitting at his table. All of a sudden, Erich shoved his beer glass aside, grabbed the fair maiden's hand, looked into her eyes, cleared his throat, and addressed his subject: "Fräulein Lulu, I must speak to you. The future public prosecutor in me prompts me to do so. And I must lodge a complaint. You are so beautiful, more beautiful than is permissible by law, that you make yourself and others unhappy. Don't try to speak in your own defense. Where is my good appetite? And my splendid thirst? Where the compendium of Corpus Juris Civilis I so laboriously crammed into my head with the help of Meisel's crib? And the Pandects? And the penal code? And civil procedures? Yes, where are they? In my head, only one paragraph remains, and its rubric reads 'Lulu.' And the footnote: 'O you lovely lady, O most lovely of them all!' "

Erich's eyes bulged even more than usual, his left hand

furiously kneaded his fashionable new silk hat to tatters, his right hand clamped down on Lulu's cool hand. She, meanwhile, was on the lookout for an opportunity to escape. Herr Müller was snoring away in the buffet; she could not call out for help.

Then, fortuitously, someone opened the door a crack; a hand and part of a white flannel shirtsleeve pushed through the narrow opening. Something white fell from the hand and fluttered to the ground; then the door closed as quickly as it had opened. Lulu managed to free herself; she bounded toward the door and retrieved the fallen piece of stationery, on which there was writing. Erich sat in vexed silence. But Lulu burst out laughing and read aloud what was on the paper:

> *Lady, must you laugh at me?*
> *See, this burning poet's head*
> *You once trusted—so you said—*
> *Now lies shamefaced at your feet.*
> *And this heart which had come to know*
> *Joy most high and Suffering most low*
> *Trembles shyly in your dainty hand.*
> *I, the wanderer, plucked red roses, and*
> *I, the singer, sang red songs for you,*
> *Now they languish, wilt, and bid adieu,*
> *Lie, poor wretches, at your feet—*
> *Must you laugh at me?*

"Lauscher!" the provoked Erich cried out. "That contemptible scoundrel! You can't possibly believe that thoughtless windbag takes his writing seriously. Those damned verses. Verses!—he writes them to a new heartthrob every three weeks!"

Lulu made no reply to Erich's outburst; she walked over to the open window and stood there listening. From outside came jangling guitar sounds, accompanied by a bass voice singing:

> *Under an impatient star*
> *I stand and play my guitar . . .*
> *Oh, do not stay and linger,*
> *But come and love your singer!*

A gust of wind set the window banging shut. At this, the innkeeper awakened in the buffet and came peevishly through the door to the main room. Erich threw his money down on the table beside his untouched beer and left the tavern without saying goodbye. Taking a leaping bound down the stairs, he went crashing into the back of the guitarist, who turned out to be none other than junior barrister Ripplein. He and Erich went off toward the chestnut-tree-lined embankment, angry and quarreling.

The lovely Lulu extinguished the gaslights in the parlor and vestibule, and went upstairs to her own room. When she passed by Lauscher's door, she could hear agitated footsteps and frequent deep, long sighs. Shaking her head, she came to her own room and lay down on her bed. Since she could not fall asleep, she mulled over the evening's events. But she no longer laughed about them; on the contrary, they made her very sad. It all now seemed like a badly played farce. Pure of heart, she wondered how all these people could be so narrow-minded and foolish, thinking only of themselves, esteeming and loving her only for her pretty face. These young men seemed like so many poor, misguided moths, reeling around a tiny flame, while she had important matters to discuss. How sad and ridiculous, all their talk about Beauty and Youth and Roses; they surrounded themselves with colorful stage sets, made entirely out of words, while the whole bitter truth of life strangely passed them by. On her simple, girlish soul the truth was plainly and deeply inscribed: the art of living inheres in learning both sorrow and laughter.

The poet Lauscher lay on his bed only half-asleep. It was a sultry night. Rash, fragmentary, feverish thoughts boiled up in his forehead and vaporized into dreams that swiftly paled; still, the extreme sultriness of the August night and the stubborn, tormenting buzzing of a few crane flies did not escape his consciousness. The crane flies tormented him most. Now they seemed to sing:

> *Perfection,*
> *Today you've peered in my direction . . .*

and now the Song of the Dream-harp. Suddenly he remembered that by now the lovely Lulu had held his poem in her hands and knew of his love. That Oscar Ripplein had serenaded her and that in all likelihood Erich, too, had confessed his love this evening was no secret to him. The poet's thoughts were filled with his beloved's enigmatic temperament, her strange unconscious tie to the philosopher Turnabout, to the Saga of Ask and to Hamelt's dream, her strangely soulful beauty and her gray, commonplace lot in life. That the whole narrow clique of the cénacle was drawn to her as to the lodestone, and that he himself —instead of taking his leave and traveling—with each passing hour found himself more and more inextricably enmeshed in the web of this romance, all this made him feel as if he and the others were merely figments of some humorist's imagination, or characters in some grotesque fable. His aching head throbbed with the notion that he and Lulu and the whole tangle of events were all textual fragments from one of the old philosopher's manuscripts, powerless and with no wills of their own; hypothetically, tentatively recombined elements in an ongoing experiment in aesthetics. And yet everything in him violently opposed such an unhappy *cogito ergo sum*; he pulled himself together, got up, and walked over to the open window. Thinking it over clearly, he recognized the hopeless absurdity of his lyrical declaration of love. He felt and understood that, at bottom, the lovely Lulu did not love him but found him laughable. Sadly he lay down on the ledge of the window; stars shone out between wisps of clouds, a breeze blew across the dark crowns of the chestnut trees. The poet decided that the next day would be his last in Kirchheim. The spirit of renunciation, both sad and uplifting, penetrated his tired, uneasy mind, which had been so befuddled with the dream of the previous day.

7

WHEN LAUSCHER WENT DOWN to the tavern early the next morning, Lulu was already busy with her chores. The two of them sat down to drink a cup of steaming hot coffee. Lulu seemed remarkably changed. An almost queenly radiance illuminated her pure, sweet face, and a singular kindness and intelligence looked out of her lovely eyes, which had grown even deeper.

"Lulu, you have become even more beautiful overnight," Lauscher said admiringly. "I didn't think such a thing possible."

Smiling, she nodded. "Yes, I've had a dream, a dream . . ."

Across the table, the poet questioned her with a look of astonishment.

"No," she said, "I cannot tell it to you."

At this moment the morning sun came in the window and shone through Lulu's dark hair, proud and golden as a halo. Attentive with sad joy, the poet's gaze hung on the exquisite image. Lulu nodded at him, smiled again, and said: "I have yet to thank you, my dear Herr Lauscher, for the poem you sent me yesterday. It was a very pretty poem, though I must confess I could not entirely understand it."

"It was such an oppressively warm night," Lauscher said, looking straight into the beauty's eyes. "May I see the poem again?"

She gave it to him. After reading it over, he folded it up and hid it away in his pocket. The lovely Lulu looked on in silence, thoughtfully nodding her head. Now they could hear the innkeeper's footsteps on the stairs. Lulu got up with a start and went back to work.

The stout little innkeeper came in and greeted Lauscher.

"Good morning to you, Herr Müller!" Hermann Lauscher replied. "This will be the last day I enjoy your hospitality; I'll be leaving tomorrow morning."

"But, Herr Lauscher, I thought . . ."

"No matter. I'd like you to put a couple of bottles of champagne on ice, and reserve the back room for tonight's farewell celebration."

"Whatever Herr Lauscher wishes."

Lauscher left the inn and set off to see Ludwig Ugel. He wanted to spend his last day in Kirchheim in the company of his best friend.

The sound of morning music already streamed from Ugel's lodgings on Steingaustrasse. His hair still uncombed, Ugel stood in his shirtsleeves at his coffee table. It was a pleasure to hear him play his fine violin. The little room was filled with sunlight.

"Is it true that you're leaving tomorrow?" Ugel asked the poet.

The latter was not a little surprised. "How do you know that?"

"Turnabout told me."

"Turnabout? The devil could learn a thing or two from him!"

"Yes, he's quite a droll companion. He spent half the night here, going on and on, quite colorfully, about some Princess, some story about a lily garden and the like. And he gave me to understand that I must rescue the Princess; he was disappointed in you, you're not the true Harp Silversong. Crazy, no? I didn't understand a word he said."

"I do," Lauscher said softly. "The old man's right."

For a while longer he listened as Ugel finished playing the interrupted sonata. As soon as he was done, the two friends left the city arm in arm and made for the Plochingen path that went through the woods. The thought of Lauscher's leaving made the two friends silent. Morning set the lovely mountains and pastures aglow with warmth. Soon the road turned and led into the deep woods; the two strollers lay down to one side of the road on a patch of cool moss.

"We ought to make a bouquet for the lovely Lulu," Ugel said, and, still lying down, began to pluck some ferns.

"Oh, yes," said the other softly, "a bouquet for the beautiful Lulu!" He uprooted a tall shrub that was covered with red blooms. "Add this to it! Red foxglove. I've nothing else to give her. Wild, fever-red, and poisonous . . ."

He said nothing more; something akin to a sob rose in his throat, bitter and sweet at the same time. Gloomily, he turned away. But Ugel put his arm around Lauscher's shoulder, turned over on his side, and with diverting gestures directed his friend's attention skyward, pointing out the wonderful play of sunlight through the bright green leaves. Each of them thought about his love, and they lay there a long time, under the sky and the treetops, in silence. A strong, cool breeze caressed their foreheads; the fateful blue sky of their carefree youth arched over their souls, perhaps for the last time. Ugel began to sing softly:

> *The Princess, fair Elisabeth—*
> *Her name is sunlight, air, and breath.*
> *Oh, that my own were such a name*
> *As would bow down to that fair dame,*
> *To Beauty, to Elisabeth,*
> *Whose own sweet scent is laden with*
> *Petals of roses, smooth and frail,*
> *Rose petals white, rose petals pale,*
> *Rimmed with evening's shimmering gold.*
> *Whoso her moist red lips so bold,*
> *Whoso her forehead clear and high*
> *Would praise in song, in pain and joy,*
> *Happy he'd be of love to die!*

The quiet sadness of the beautiful hour made his friend's bosom heave with pleasure and pain. He closed his eyes. From deep within his soul, the image of the lovely Lulu arose, just as he'd seen her that morning, transfigured by sunlight—mild, luminous, intelligent, and unapproachable. His heart throbbed in agitation and grief. Sighing, he ran his fingers over his brow; absently he tore at the foxglove, and sang:

> *I would bow down before you*
> *As gentle suitor should,*
> *In songs I would adore you*
> *Red as roses and red as blood.*

I wish to make obeisance,
As knight be understood,
And pledge you my allegiance,
With roses red as blood.

To you, my saint, I offer
This prayer, on bended knee,
This song of love. Pray suffer
To hear my solemn plea.

He had scarcely finished singing when, from deep in the woods, the philosopher Turnabout called out to them. The two recumbent friends looked up to see him emerge from the bushes.

"Good day," he called out as he approached. "Good day, my friends! Add this to your bouquet for the lovely Lulu!" So saying, he placed a huge, white lily in Lauscher's hand. Then he comfortably settled down on a mossy rock opposite the two friends.

"Tell us, Sorcerer," Lauscher addressed him, "since you seem both ubiquitous and omniscient, tell us who the lovely Lulu really is."

"That's quite a question!" the graybeard smirked. "She herself does not know. That she's the stepsister of that accursed Frau Müller you probably don't believe, nor do I. She knew neither her father nor her mother, and her only tie to home is a strophe of a remarkable song in which she calls a certain King Sorrowless 'Father.'"

"Poppycock!" Ugel snapped.

"How so, my dear sir?" the old man answered appeasingly. "Be that as it may, certain secrets are best left undisturbed . . . I hear, Herr Lauscher, that you intend to leave us and go abroad tomorrow. What an enormous capacity people have for self-deception! I would have wagered you'd be staying around these parts longer, since, so it seems to me, you and Lulu . . ."

"That's quite enough," Lauscher interrupted him, flaring up. "Why the devil should other people's love affairs be your concern!"

"Calm yourself," the philosopher replied, with a pacifying smile. "My esteemed fellow, I had no intention of speaking of such affairs. That I concern myself with the intricacies of certain peculiar fates, and especially with the fates of poets, is entirely natural; it's part and parcel of my science. I have absolutely no doubt that some very subtile, magical ties that bind you to our Lulu have arisen; even if, as I surmise, at the present time certain insuperable obstacles prevent a favorable outcome."

"Please do explain yourself a bit more clearly," the poet replied, standoffish, but still curious.

The old man shrugged his shoulders. "Well now," he said, "each and every human Soul that exists on a higher plane instinctively strives for that Harmony which inheres in the happy balance of the Conscious and the Unconscious. However, as long as the Cognitive Self takes, as its life principle, a destructive Dualism, these striving temperaments tend to ally themselves—through only half-understood instinct—with temperaments whose striving directly opposes their own. Now understand me. Such bonds can be formed without words or knowledge; like affinities, they can arise unrecognized and have their life and effect solely through the Emotions. In any case, they are predetermined and stand outside the sphere of Personal Volition. They are an immeasurably important element of that which we call Fate. It so happens that the proper and actual benefits of such a bond can only be reaped at the moment of separation and renunciation; these being subject to our Will, over which this affinity has no power."

"I do understand you," said Lauscher in a completely different tone. "It seems you are my friend, Herr Turnabout!"

"Did you ever doubt it?" The other smiled merrily.

"You must come to my farewell party tonight at the Crown!"

"So we shall see, Herr Lauscher. According to certain calculations, tonight an old problem of mine should be resolved, an old dream be fulfilled . . . But perhaps this can be combined with your party. *Auf Wiedersehen!*" He jumped to his feet, waved goodbye, and quickly disappeared on the road leading to the valley.

The friends stayed in the woods until noon, both of them thinking about Lauscher's departure, each one filled with his love and a host of conflicting emotions. They arrived late for the midday meal at the Crown. But they found Lulu in a gay mood, wearing a bright, new dress. She cheerfully accepted the flowers and put them in a vase on the corner table at which she served them their meal. Her lovely figure moved about, happy and industrious, bringing and taking away plates, bowls, and bottles. After the meal, she joined them for a glass of wine; plans for Lauscher's farewell party were the topic of conversation.

"We must get everything ready for the party; this room needs decorating," said Lulu. "As you can see, I've taken the first step myself, putting on this brand-new dress. We could use some flowers . . ."

"We'll see to that right away," Ugel interrupted.

"Good," she said, smiling. "A few Chinese lanterns, and some colored ribbons would be nice as well."

"As many as you like!" Ugel called out again. Lauscher nodded in silence.

"You're awfully quiet, Herr Lauscher," Lulu said, annoyed. "Have you any objections?"

Lauscher made no reply. While his gaze hung on her slender figure and lovely countenance, all he could say was: "How beautiful you are today, Lulu." And again: "How beautiful you are!"

He was insatiable, he had to look again and again at her breathtaking image. Watching her and his friend make arrangements for his departure pained him beyond description and made him silent and gloomy. Every moment, a bitter and tormenting thought repeatedly occurred to him: that his renunciation and departure were not to be. He had to throw himself at her feet, to encircle her with all the burning flames of his passion, to woo and win her, to take her by force and ravish her. To do something, anything but sit idly by in her presence, while one blessed moment after another of his last hours in it hastily and irretrievably ran out. Nonetheless, he fought bitterly to gain control over his emotions, and in these last moments he concentrated on one thing: to impress her beautiful image deep into his soul, until it was branded there, glowing and painful, as desire never to be forgotten.

Finally, when the three were alone in the room and Ugel was pressing to leave, Lauscher got up, walked up to Lulu, and clasped her hand in his own hot, trembling hand. Then he said softly, in a forced, festively comic tone: "My beautiful Princess, may it please Your Majesty graciously to accept my offer of service! Regard me, I beg of you, as your knight, your slave, your dog, your fool; your wish is my command . . ."

"Good, my knight," Lulu broke in, smiling. "I do require a service of you. Tonight I need a glad-hearted companion and buffoon, one who can help me make a certain party entertaining and pleasant. Will you accept this task?"

Lauscher turned very white. Then he let out a harsh laugh and with comic exaggeration got down on his knees and spoke with pompous solemnity: "I do so promise, most noble lady!"

Then he and Ludwig Ugel hurried off. First they went to the horticulturist near the cemetery, and raged with merciless shears through the proprietor's rose garden. Lauscher especially was not to be restrained. "I must have a huge basket full of white roses," he cried repeatedly, leaving no branch untrimmed, shearing off dozens and dozens of his favorite flower for the lovely Lulu. Then he paid the gardener, told him to bring the roses to the Crown that evening, and sauntered off through the town with Ugel. Whenever they saw something bright or colorful in a shop window, they stormed in and made their purchases: fans, scarfs, silk ribbons, paper lanterns, and finally some small fireworks that would still make a fine display. Back at the Crown, the lovely Lulu had her hands full with receiving and arranging all these effects. But, unknown to anyone, the good Turnabout helped her until evening.

8

LULU WAS EVEN more beautiful and more gay than ever. Lauscher and Ugel had finished their supper; one after another, their friends arrived at the inn. When they had all gathered together, following Lauscher—who gracefully led Lulu on his arm—they proceeded into the back room. Its walls were covered with scarfs, ribbons, and garlands. From the ceiling hung row upon row of colorful lanterns, every one of them lit. The large table was spread with a white cloth, set with champagne glasses, and strewn with fresh roses. The poet presented his lady with the philosopher's lily, put a half-opened tea rose in her hair, and escorted her to the place of honor. Everyone was in good cheer and sat down with some commotion; the evening was inaugurated with a choral song. Now the corks flew from the bottles; frothing over, the bright noble wine flowed into the fragile glasses, and Erich Tänzer made the champagne toast. Jokes were answered with laughter; Turnabout's late arrival was hailed with thunderous applause; Ugel and

Lauscher each recited a few charming verses. Then the lovely Lulu sang this song:

> *A King once lay in prison*
> *In deep and dark distress—*
> *But now he is arisen*
> *The King called Sorrowless.*
>
> *And now bright lights are gleaming*
> *Throughout the happy land,*
> *And now glad poems are streaming*
> *From every poet's hand.*
>
> *More white and red than ever*
> *Lilies and roses bloom;*
> *Silversong's harpstrings quiver*
> *With its most sacred song.*

When the song ended, Lauscher dug deep into the basket of roses, and applauding the singer, he threw handful after handful of white roses her way. Then a merry war was declared: roses flew from seat to seat, in dozens, in hundreds, white roses, red roses; old Turnabout's hair and gray beard were completely covered with them. It was nearly midnight; Turnabout stood up and made a speech:

"Dear Friends and Beautiful Lulu! We can all see that the reign of King Sorrowless has begun anew. Even I must say farewell today, but not without the hope that I may see you all again; for my King, into whose service I return, is a friend to the young and to poets. Were you philosophers, I would tell you all a mystical allegory about the Rebirth of the Beautiful, and especially about the Salvation of the Poetic Principle through the ironic Metamorphosis of Mythos, the happy ending of which you will soon come to know. But, as things are, I shall present the denouement of this Askian tale in pleasing pictures before your very eyes. Let the play go on!"

All eyes followed his index finger to a huge, embroidered curtain that closed off one corner of the room. The curtain was suddenly illuminated from within, revealing a weft of innumerable silver lilies framing the marble basin of a gushing fountainhead. The art of the textile and of the lighting was so fine that the lilies could be seen growing, swaying, interlacing, and the spring plashing and gushing; yes, one could definitely hear the cool rush of its noble waters.

All eyes were fixed on the splendid curtain, so no one noticed that every lantern in the room, one after another, quickly went out. Everyone was deeply engrossed in the magical play of the artificial lilies; only the poet paid it no mind. Through the darkness he raised his glowing eyes and turned them beseechingly on the lovely Lulu. Her face was bathed in a solemnly beautiful and delicate light; in her magnificent dark hair the white rose shimmered with an unearthly sheen.

In unspeakable harmony, the slender lilies circled round the fountain in a wonderfully strange ring dance. Their fine movements and delicate interweaving caught the senses of the breathless onlookers in a sweet, dreamy net of wonder and pleasure. Then a clock struck twelve. Quick as a flash, the resplendent curtain went up; a broad stage loomed in deep twilight. The philosopher got up; the movement of his chair could be heard in the darkness. He vanished and in the same instant appeared on the stage, his hair and beard still full of roses. Gradually, the stage filled with a light that grew stronger and stronger, until the curtain's wellspring and lilies—brilliantly clear—could distinctly be seen plashing and blooming in noble reality.

In the midst of it all stood the faithful Haderbart, recognizably Turnabout, despite his transfigured mien. In the background, fascinating in its pearl-blue beauty, the Opal Palace towered. Through its broad, vaulted windows you could see the great banquet hall, and there King Sorrowless, in perfect serenity, sat on his throne. While the radiance grew ever stronger, Haderbart, carrying an enormous, fabulous silver harp, made his way through the obeisant lilies to the center of the stage. The splendor was now blinding and broke over the walls of the Opal Palace in feverishly trembling waves, silvery and iridescent.

Poised to listen, the faithful Haderbart plucked one single deep string of the harp. A clear, kingly tone rang out and swelled. Slowly the lilies in the foreground stepped to the side; a splendid staircase dropped from the stage to the floor. In the dark room, tall and slender, the beautiful Lulu arose, and as she climbed the stairs they vanished behind her. Finally she stood there, the figure of the Princess, beautiful beyond words. Bowing deeply, Haderbart gave the harp into her hands; tears flowed from his clear, old eyes and fell, along with one of the roses loosed from his beard, to the ground.

Tall and resplendent, the Princess stood at the Harp Silversong. Making a sweeping gesture toward the palace, her right arm drew the harp toward her until it rested against her shoulder. Then her slender fingers swept over all its strings, from which issued a song of unprecedented bliss and harmony. All the tall lilies gathered round their mistress to pay homage. Once again, a pure, full chord sounded on the reverberating magical strings—then with a brief thud the curtain fell. One moment longer it remained wholly lit from within; the passionate dance of the embroidered lilies grew faster and more furious, until all that could be discerned was a single, silver whirlpool, which suddenly and soundlessly foundered in utter darkness.

The friends remained standing or sitting in the darkness, stupefied and speechless. But soon enough they began to recover their senses. Lights were lit. Inadvertently, the forgotten fireworks were set off and exploded with a horrible din. Screaming and scolding, the innkeeper and his wife rushed in. A nightwatchman in the street battered on the locked shutters with his stick. In the general confusion, questions and screams were volleyed back and forth.

But no one could find a trace of Lulu or the philosopher. Junior barrister Ripplein grew irritable and began to speak of trickery; but no one listened to him. Hermann Lauscher had escaped to his room and bolted the door from inside.

When, very early the next morning, Lauscher set out on his journey, still no trace had been found of the beautiful Lulu. Because he immediately left for parts unknown, we cannot expect his report on the subsequent course of events in Kirchheim. But it is to him we owe the above account, transcribed in strict accordance with the facts.

Hannes

I N A SMALL TOWN lived a well-to-do artisan who had
twice been married. From his first marriage he had a
son who was strong and brutal; but his second son, Hannes,
was a delicate boy, who from early on was taken to be
somewhat simpleminded.

After his mother's death, hard times came upon Hannes;
his brother despised and mistreated him, and his father
always sided with the elder brother, for it disgraced him
to have such a stupid son. Because he took no part in the
pleasures and activities of other boys, spoke very little, and
put up with quite a lot, Hannes gradually gained the reputation of being an extremely dull-witted child. And since
he no longer had recourse to his mother, he had gotten
into the habit of strolling about the meadows and gardens
outside the town gate, whenever he was free to leave his
father's house.

Sometimes he stayed out there half the day, taking
pleasure in examining the plants and flowers, learning to
distinguish the many classes of stones, birds, beetles, and
other animals; and he was on the best of terms with all
these things and creatures. In these pursuits he was often
quite alone, but not always. Small children not infrequently
sought out his company, and it became apparent that al-

though Hannes had nothing at all in common with boys of his own age, he made friends easily with many of the younger children. He showed them where the flowers grew, he played with them and told them stories; when they were tired he carried them, when they quarreled he made peace between them.

At first people did not like to see the young ones following him around. Then they grew accustomed to the sight, and many mothers were happy to sometimes leave their children in the boy's care.

Yet, in a few years' time, Hannes would suffer unpleasantness at the hands of his former charges. As soon as they outgrew his guardianship and heard from someone what a simpleton Hannes was, the well-bred avoided him, and the coarse mocked him.

When this became too painful for him to bear, he would escape alone to the gardens or the woods and would lure goats with vegetables or birds with crumbs, cheering himself with the company of the trees and animals, from which he need have no fear of disloyalty or enmity. He saw God travel across the earth atop high thunderclouds, he saw the Saviour wander on the still field paths, and when he saw Him, he would hide himself in the bushes and wait, with pounding heart, until He passed by.

When the time came for him to take up a profession, he did not go to work in his father's workshop as his brother had done, but rather he left the town for the farms and worked as a herdsman. He drove sheep and goats, swine and cattle, and even geese to pasture. No harm came to his animals, and soon they knew and loved him; recognizing his call, they followed him in preference to other herdsmen. Townspeople and farmers alike were quick to notice this, and after a few years they entrusted their best and finest herds to the young herdsman. But when he had to go to market in town, his gait was humble and shy; the apprentices teased him, the schoolchildren called him names, and his brother, refusing to acknowledge him, contemptuously turned his back on him. When their father fell victim to an epidemic, his brother cheated him out of more than half his inheritance; Hannes paid it no mind and made no protest. Whatever he saved of his herdsman's wages he sometimes gave to children or the poor, more often he would buy a collar with a bright bell for a cow or goat that he loved better than the others.

And so, many years went by; Hannes was no longer young. He knew very little of the life of men, but he knew quite a lot about wind and weather, livestock and dogs, the way the grass grows and the crops ripen. He could distinguish every one of his animals by its beauty and strength, by its disposition and age; moreover, he could identify all kinds of birds, knowing their habits and species; he also knew lizards, snakes, beetles, bees, flies, pine martens, and squirrels. He understood plants and herbs, soil and water, the seasons, and the phases of the moon. He settled disputes and put an end to jealousy among his animals, tended and healed them when they were sick, carefully raised those orphaned at birth, and never gave a thought to being anything other than a herdsman.

One day, while Hannes lay in the shade at the edge of the woods minding his cattle, a woman came running from the town into the woods; though she came quite near Hannes, she did not see him. Because she appeared to be in great distress, Hannes kept an eye on her, and soon he saw that she intended to take her own life, for she was tying a rope to the branch of a beech tree and was about to place the noose around her neck.

Cautiously but quickly, Hannes approached her, laid his hand on her shoulder, and put a stop to her plan. Terrified, the woman paused and gave him a hostile look. Then he obliged her to sit, and by speaking to her as one speaks to an inconsolable child, he brought her around; she told him her troubles and her whole story. She said she could no longer live with her husband, but Hannes could hear and sense quite clearly that she was still fond of him. He let her go on about her troubles until she calmed down a little. Then he tried to console her; he spoke of other things, his work, the woods and the herds, and finally he implored her to return home and try once more to talk to her husband. Weeping softly, she walked away, and for quite some time he neither saw nor heard anything more from her.

But, as autumn approached, the woman returned with her husband and his brother. She was happy and thankful; she told the herdsman the story of their reconciliation, invited him to visit them in town; and pointing to her brother-in-law, she asked Hannes not to deny counsel and consolation to him as well. The brother-in-law told Hannes his troubles: his mill had burned down and a son had died in the fire. Enormous serenity and strength dwelled in the shepherd as he looked at, listened to, and consoled the man. Without being conscious of it, he comforted the man and gave him new strength to live. With thanks, the townspeople left their comforter.

It was not long before the woman's brother-in-law came to Hannes, bringing along a friend in need of advice; this friend later returned with still another. And, after a few years had passed, the whole town spoke of the shepherd Hannes's ability to heal the sick-in-spirit, to settle disputes, to counsel the disconsolate, and give hope to those in despair.

As always, there were many who scoffed at him, but almost every day some new petitioner sought him out. He led a young spendthrift and ne'er-do-well back onto the path of virtue; he bestowed patience and hope on those who were sorely distressed; and a great stir went up when the differences between two rich families were reconciled through his mediation.

Many people spoke of superstition and sorcery; but since the shepherd took payment from no one, all reproaches were dispelled; people went to seek the unassuming man's advice as if seeking the blessing of a saintly hermit. Legends and tales about his person and his life were popular everywhere; it was said that the beasts of the field followed him and that he understood the language of the birds, that he could make rain fall and divert the course of lightning.

His elder brother was foremost among those who still

spoke of Hannes with scorn and envy. He called him a fool and a fool-catcher, and one evening, while carousing, he vowed to take his brother to task and put an end to his activities. True to his word, the next day he set off with two companions to find his brother. On an out-of-the-way moor, Hannes received him graciously, offered him bread and milk, inquired as to the health and well-being of himself and his family. And, before the elder brother could utter even one ill word, the herdsman's nature touched and soothed him so greatly that he begged his forgiveness and contritely made his way home.

This last story stopped all malicious tongues from wagging; it was told again and again, each time with new details, and a young man wrote a poem about it.

When Hannes reached the age of fifty-five, the town fell on evil days. Senseless disputes broke out among the citizenry, blood flowed, and fierce hostilities arose. Poisoning was rumored to be the cause of certain unexplained deaths. And, while the community was still immersed in passionate factionalism, a horrifying pestilence spread through the region; first it brought death to children, then it struck down adults, and in a few weeks one-fourth of the population was swept off.

And, amidst these bad times, the old town burgomaster died. Now despondency and desperation gained the upper hand in a municipality afflicted with sickness and civil discord. Bands of thieves imperiled everyone's well-being, all but the rogues had lost their heads, threatening letters terrorized the rich, and the poor had nothing to eat.

Hannes

Looking for some of his protégés, Hannes came into town one day. He found one dead, another ill, a third orphaned and impoverished; houses stood empty, and in the streets terror, anxiety, and suspicion reigned. Hannes's soul ached with the misery of his native town; and while he crossed the marketplace, several people in the crowd recognized him. A swarm of people, all in need of help, followed close behind him and would not let him get away. Without knowing how it came to pass, Hannes found himself on the uppermost step in front of the Town Hall, suddenly faced with a huge throng of people thirsty for words of consolation and hope.

Then an impulse to soothe and console them came over him; he stretched out his arms and spoke to the people, and they began to grow calm. He told them of sickness and death, sin and redemption, and he ended with a consoling tale. Yesterday, he said to them, on the hill above the town, he had seen Jesus, the Saviour of the World, who was on His way to put an end to all misery. And, while he spoke of this, his face beamed with compassion and love, and many wanted to believe that Hannes was the Redeemer sent by God to save them.

"Bring Him here!" cried the crowd. "Bring us the Saviour, that He may help us!"

Only now did Hannes begin to feel the terrible power and force of the intemperate hopes he had aroused. His senses clouded over and grew weary; for the first time in his life, he felt the misery of the world to be greater and more powerful than the power of his faith. The unfortunate ones who stood before him were no longer content to hear about the Saviour; so as not to doubt, they wanted to see Him themselves, to grasp His hands and hear His voice.

"I will pray to Him for you," he said in a strained voice. "For three days and three nights I will seek Him out and implore Him to return with me to help you."

Tired and confused, the prophet made his way through the swarming multitude; he crossed the bridge, went through the gate, and reached open ground, where the last few followers left him. Sorrowfully he entered the forest and with heavy thoughts he sought out that spot where at other times he sometimes had felt the nearness of God. Praying, but without hope, he went astray, oppressed by the misery of thousands. Without desiring it, he, a herdsman and friend of children, had become a spiritual adviser for the many; he had helped many and saved many, and now all this had been to no avail, and he was made to see that evil was inextinguishable and triumphant on earth.

On the fourth day, he entered the town slowly, bent over; his face had grown old, his hair had turned white. The people waited for him in silence, and many of them knelt down as he passed by.

He ended his life with a lie, which, nonetheless, was the truth.

"Have you seen God? And what has He told you?" the people asked.

And he opened his eyes and answered them: "This is what He told me: 'Get you hence and die for your town, as I have died for the world.' "

Hannes

For a while fear and disappointment held the multitude captive. Then an old man jumped to his feet, cursing, and spit in the prophet's face. And so Hannes met his end, and in silence succumbed to the wrath of the people.

The Merman

FROM AN OLD CHRONICLE

DESPITE THE SPREAD of humanism in Italy in the early years of the fifteenth century, many more things which defy rational explanation came to pass between Milan and Naples in those day than in ours; in any case, the chroniclers of that time, despite their occasional sophistication, were constantly opening their eyes wide in astonishment and telling, with candor befitting their vocation, of wholly curious matters. One such incident from that time, supported by the testimony of numerous eyewitnesses, is the following.

A seaside city, to be sure not very large, but very old, widely celebrated, and inhabited by any number of men who were a credit to the arts and sciences, erected a lovely church on the site where long before had stood a temple to Neptune. The building was completed and consecrated, and was admired, with pride and joy, by all who saw it— all, that is, but the jealous inhabitants of the neighboring town.

A short time after the bishop had consecrated the church, a hideous storm blew up and raged with unprecedented fierceness for four days and nights. Several fishing barques went down with all hands; a sailing ship carrying precious cargo sank not far from the coast; and the enormously heavy, gold-plated cross was torn from the steeple of the newly built church. It plummeted through the roof of the church and hung, ruined and bent out of shape, in the rafters. To many, its present form appeared to be that of a trident, and they concluded therefore that this was an act of vengeance by the outraged God of the Sea. Others took pains to demonstrate the untenability of this assertion; it became a matter of heated debate, and soon the whole city was up in arms about it. In the council chamber, the great historian Marcus Salestris delivered a treatise on the nature and history of the divinity of the sea god, a thorough piece of work, full of citations of and allusions to the works of the ancients and of the church fathers, which culminated in the conviction that the sea gods of former times had been either eradicated or else plunged into the unknown and desolate ocean on the other side of the continent.

The famous orator Caesarius answered him in a public address. While acknowledging Salestris's erudition and merits, he firmly maintained the opposing point of view; and to many people his view was exceedingly plausible, for he enumerated many instances—both from the chronicles and from the logbooks of sailors of more recent times —of encounters between human beings and heathen sea creatures.

In the meantime, the terrible storm had abated, and when the sea had properly calmed down, fishermen and other people whose livelihood depended on it could again ply their trades on the shore.

Then one morning fishwives came running into the city; screaming aloud, they brought the news: a naked man, half covered with seaweed, had been washed ashore. They had supposed it was the corpse of a man who had died in the storm, and soon a large band of people—some ready to help, others merely curious—accompanied them to the shore. They brought along poles, nets, and ropes; some of them set their boats on the water; and thus they neared the body, which, not far from the beach, appeared to be caught in creeping seaweed and was bobbing up and down in time with the breakers which engulfed it. Women wailed and prayed; youths and children looked with horror upon the pale, shimmering body, now exposed to the breast, now showing only a hand over the water.

Because of the uncertainty of the sea floor and the numerous shoals, it was found advisable to haul in the body by means of a dragnet attached to three boats. Experienced men set out and accomplished their task.

But it was with horror that the throng of onlookers cried out as they saw the body suddenly and violently move in the net that surrounded it. Thrashing its arms, it tore at the net, and unexpectedly let out such a savage and hideous roar that every heart froze in terror. At the same time, he hurled himself, as if in spasm, high up into the air, and now all could see that the creature was equipped with a powerful fish tail in place of legs.

"A monster! A merman! A sea monster!" they cried out

in confusion, and not a few ran away. But the men in the boats, though terrified, stood their ground and with superior strength pulled the inextricably entangled creature onto dry land. There they tied up the netted creature with heavy ropes, threw him into a two-wheeled cart, and conveyed him, amid the monstrous hue and cry of the people, into the city.

Meantime, those who had already fled had brought the news to every street and lane, and just as the men hurried the cart into the marketplace, a huge throng of people streamed in from all directions.

"Kill him!" "Draw and quarter him!" hundreds of voices cried out. Yet no one dared approach the prisoner, over whom his captors stood guard.

Men of name and esteem turned out in good numbers, along with the mayor, and there was much heated discussion among them. The historian Salestris and the orator Caesarius, having in mind closer observation, were the first to approach the monster, who lay in the wagon. No matter how widely their opinions diverged, they were, nevertheless, of one mind in this matter: every attempt must be made to keep the stranger alive. And they prevailed against the wishes of the multitude, enabling the men who had delivered the prisoner to throw him— bound as he was—into the fountain in the marketplace, and he immediately sank beneath the water's surface.

The fountain was garrisoned with sentries, and the overwrought townspeople prowled around the square for some time. Meanwhile, in the Town Hall, in consultation with the learned men, deliberations went on as to what further steps were to be taken. Salestris and Caesarius were granted permission and enjoined to study the triton as closely as they could; and, if at all possible, they were to speak with him.

They went to the fountain, where the guards shielded them from the thronging crowd of the curious. The merman lay at the bottom of the deep stone basin, and only after several hours did they succeed in luring him to the surface with bread and fish. Finally he emerged, and it was evident that in the interim he had managed to extricate himself from the net and lines. The two scholars made the sign of the cross, which provoked laughter from the merman. Then, first the one, then the other, spoke to him, in Italian and in Latin. But he did not understand them, though he seemed to listen intently and to take pains to respond partly through gesture, partly through the incomprehensible sounds of a foreign tongue.

A second session in the Town Hall was inconclusive. Caesarius expressed his conviction that it had to be possible to communicate with the stranger in some language or other. And so a southern sailor was found, one who lived in town as the manager of a shipping office, and who was fluent in the language of the Saracens. He, too, spoke to the monster and was not understood. But it struck him as plausible that the monster was speaking Greek, since the sounds the creature made were very like those of the Greek language, which, to be sure, he himself did not understand, but which he had sometimes heard spoken at sea.

It was now a matter of finding someone who knew Greek. And yet there was no one at hand, for at that time knowledge of the Greek language was not at all widespread. Still, the historian Salestris knew that one Doctor Charikles, a resident of the neighboring town, had in his possession books written in Greek and was given to boasting of his Greek studies. But no one wanted to fetch Charikles and thereby bestow favor on the detested neighboring town.

Late in the evening, however, in a final session of the town council, it was deemed proper to bring in the foreign doctor and scholar in secret; and Caesarius accepted the task, albeit reluctantly. Early the next morning he mounted his horse and rode to the town, which lay at no great distance; he called on Charikles, flattered him greatly, and bade him, finally, to accompany him without causing a sensation. Charikles replied that he had not the slightest intention of rendering a service to the enemy of his own town; nonetheless, in the interests of science, and for a suitable reward, he would, for all that, accompany Caesarius.

And so, in the late afternoon, the noblemen, the scholars, and the doctor Charikles stood by the edge of the fountain basin. The sea monster emerged and, using both arms, set himself on the stone breastwork. Charikles spoke to him in Latin and in Italian, but with no result. Then he began to speak Greek, and scarcely had he uttered a few sentences when the monster, too, started making unfamiliar sounds. "Good," said the doctor to the bystanders. "He is answering me." "But it seems to me," Salestris opined, "that the monster is not speaking the same language as you, sir." "You have a keen ear," rejoined the foreigner, smiling. "The triton speaks Greek all right, but it is an ancient Ionian dialect, the same one in which the Homeric songs are composed."

He continued to speak to the monster, until the latter, tired of the effort, dived into the water and disappeared. Thereupon Charikles read his conversation into the protocol in the Town Hall. According to this testimony, the merman had reported that he was an emissary of the god Poseidon. The god was angry that a temple to a strange god had been erected on the site of his former temple; for that reason he had sent the storm, destroyed fishermen, sailors, and their goods, and damaged the steeple and roof of the new temple. Should the inhabitants of the town be so bold as to repair the damages, his vengeance would know no bounds. Furthermore, he demanded as propitiation that his likeness be set on the pillar of the fountain in the marketplace.

Charikles received a fitting reward and was accompanied halfway back to his town by two noblemen. That night the sea monster three times let out a hideous cry and was gone without a trace the next morning. Shortly thereafter, a bronze likeness of Neptune was placed over the fountain, and the hole in the roof of the new church went unrepaired, letting in both sunshine and rain. This contributed to the rapid deterioration of the building; that church is not the one standing today, for in the seventeenth century it was replaced by another, in the baroque style.

The Enamored Youth

A LEGEND

THIS NARRATIVE REFERS to events which took place in the days of Saint Hilarion. In the town where he was born, near Gaza, there lived a simple, pious couple whom the Lord had blessed with a daughter of intelligence and great beauty. Reared by her parents in the ways of goodness, the sensitive girl, to everyone's delight, grew in humility and piety, and was, in all her discreet charm, as lovely to behold as an angel of God. Her dark, shining hair played about her white forehead; long, velvety-black lashes shaded her modestly lowered eyes; she walked on tiny, delicate feet, slender and light as the gazelles under the palm trees. She would not even look at men, for in her fourteenth year of age she had taken deathly ill, and she had vowed—should He save her—to take none but God as husband, and God had accepted her offering.

A youth who lived in the same town fell in love with this picture of undefiled maiden chastity. He, too, was handsome and comely, the son of well-to-do parents, who had bred and raised him with all due care. But once he had fallen in love with the lovely young woman, he would do nothing but seek out every opportunity to see her; and when he did, he would stand enraptured before the ever so lovely child, gazing at her with ardent yearning in his eyes. When a day would pass without his seeing her face, he would mope around pale and dejected, eat nothing, and pass many an hour in sighs and lamentations.

Having had a good, Christian upbringing, the youth was possessed of a gentle and pious temperament, but now this violent infatuation reigned over his heart and soul. He was no longer able to pray, and instead of meditating on the holy things, he thought only of the maiden's long, black hair, her tranquil, beautiful eyes, the color and contours of her cheeks and lips, her slender, shining neck, and her tiny agile feet. But he was reluctant to let her know of his great love and eager desire; for he knew only too well that she meant to take no earthly husband, bearing no love within her but to God and to her parents.

Languishing with lovesickness, he finally wrote her a long, imploring letter in which he declared his ardent love; with all his heart he begged her to accept him, and, in days to come, to live with him in holy matrimony, as would please God. He scented his missive with a noble Persian powder, rolled it up, tied it with a silken cord, and secretly sent it to her by the hands of an old maidservant.

When the maiden read his words, she turned scarlet. In the first flush of confusion, her inclination was to tear the letter to pieces or show it immediately to her mother. But then, she had known and liked the youth well as a child, and in his words she perceived a certain diffidence and tenderness, so she did no such thing; instead, she gave the letter back to the old woman, saying: "Return this letter to him who has written it, and tell him that he may never again address such words to me. Tell him also that by my parents I have been promised as a bride to God; thus, I may never offer my hand to any man, but shall stand firm in my resolve to serve and honor Him in virginal purity, for love unto Him is higher and worthier than human love. Further, tell him that I hope not to find even one man whose love is higher and worthier than God's, and so I would persist in my solemn vow. To him who has written this letter I wish God's peace, which surpasseth all understanding. And now get you hence and know that never again shall I accept such a message from your hands."

Astonished at such steadfastness of purpose, the maidservant returned to her master, brought him his letter, and reported all that the maiden had said.

Although she added several consoling words, the youth burst out in loud lamentations, rent his garments, and cast dirt upon his head. He no longer dared cross the maiden's path, and sought to catch sight of her only from a distance. Nights he lay sleepless in his chamber, crying aloud the name of his beloved, and a hundred fond terms of endearment; he called her his Light and his Star, his Roe Deer and his Palm, his Eyebright and his Pearl, and when he awakened from these reveries to find himself alone in the dark room, he clenched his teeth, cursed the name of God, and battered his head against the wall.

This earthly love had eclipsed and extinguished all

piety in his heart. And scarcely had the Devil gained entry than he hurled the youth from one abomination to another. The youth took an oath that he would have the lovely girl for himself, and would do so by force. He journeyed to Memphis, where he entered the school of the heathen priests of Asklepios, and took instruction in the arts of sorcery. He zealously pursued these studies for a year before returning home to Gaza.

Upon his return, he incised on a copper tablet signs and words of power to induce a strong love charm. In the dark of night, he buried the tablet under the threshold of the house in which the maiden lived.

Even on the very next day, the girl was remarkably changed. She gave free reign to her once so modestly lowered gaze; she loosed her hair and let it fall freely; she neglected her prayers and failed to attend divine services, and to herself she sang a little love song which no one had taught her. Daily her condition grew more serious, and nightly she tossed and turned in her bed, crying aloud the youth's name, calling him her most dearly beloved, desiring him near.

Her much-altered condition could not long remain concealed from the bewitched girl's parents. Having become suspicious of her changed words and manners, they listened in on her at night, and were so shocked and horrified at what they heard that the father wanted to disown his ill-bred daughter, as he called her. The mother, however, begged him to have patience; they began to examine the matter more closely and recognized that their daughter must have fallen into such a sad state of confusion owing to the influence of a magic spell.

But the maiden remained possessed of a demon, spewing blasphemies and calling out loudly for her beloved. At long last, her parents remembered the saintly hermit Hilarion, who for many years had lived in a desolate spot far from the town and who was so close to God that all his prayers were heard. He had healed so many sick and had cast out so many devils that, next to Saint Anthony, he could perhaps be called the most powerful holy man of his day. They brought their daughter to him, and while telling him all that had come to pass, they implored him to heal her.

The saint turned to the maiden and bellowed: "Who has made of God's handmaid a vessel of unholy lust?" But the girl, her body shrunken, her skin ashen, looked at him and began to revile him, boasting of her white skin and her sleek body, calling the man of God a scabious scarecrow, so that her poor parents sank down on their knees and hid their heads in shame. But Hilarion, recognizing the demon that resided in the girl, smiled and launched a vigorous attack, so that it acknowledged its name and confessed all. Forcefully, the saint exorcised the violently contentious demon from the maiden. Then she awakened, as if out of some feverish dream, recognized and greeted her weeping parents, asked Hilarion for his blessing, and was, from that moment on, the same pious bride to God she had been before.

The young man had been waiting for the charm to

overpower the maiden and thrust her into his arms. He spent several days secure in his hope, during which time the things related with respect to the maiden had come to pass. Already healed, she had returned to the town, and as the youth was crossing the street, he saw her coming from afar and walked toward her. As she came nearer, he could see that her forehead again glowed with its former purity; over her face such a peaceful beauty spread that she seemed to be coming directly from paradise. Perplexed, the youth hung back, having begun, the moment he saw her, to feel ashamed of the sacrilege he had committed. But he defended himself against it, and when she came close by him, he put his trust in the efficacy of the charm, went over to her, took hold of her hand, and said: "Now do you love me?"

Without blushing, the maiden raised her pure eyes, which shone on him like stars. An ineffable loving kindness radiated from them. She pressed his hand and said: "Yes, my brother, I love you. I love your poor soul, and I beg of you, deliver it from evil, and give it into God's keeping, so that it can again be beautiful and pure."

An invisible hand touched the youth's heart. His eyes brimmed with tears, and he cried: "Oh, must I renounce you forever? But give me a command, I will do naught but what you bid me."

She smiled like an angel and said to him: "You need not renounce me forever. There will come a day when we will stand before God's throne. Let us prepare ourselves for that day so that we can look Him in the face and endure His judgment. Then I will be your friend. It is but for a short time that we must remain apart."

Gently he let go her hand, and smiling she walked away. For a while he stood like one under a spell, then he too walked on, locked up his house, and went into the wilderness to serve God. His beauty left him; he grew thin and brown and shared his dwelling with the beasts of the field. And when he grew weary and suffered doubt and could find no other consolation, he would endlessly repeat her words: "It is but for a short time . . ."

And probably the time seemed long to him; he grew gray and white and stayed on the earth even into his eighty-first year. What are a mere eighty years? The ages flee and are gone, as if on the wings of a bird. Since the days of that youth, one thousand and several hundred years have gone by, and how soon, too, will our names and deeds be forgotten, and no more trace of our life remain than perhaps a short, uncertain legend . . .

Three Lindens

MORE THAN a hundred years ago, in the green cemetery of the Hospital of the Holy Ghost in Berlin, there stood three splendid old linden trees. They were so big that the branches and boughs of their gigantic crowns had grown tangled into one another, and they arched over the entire cemetery like one enormous roof. The origin of these beautiful lindens, however, lies several centuries further back and is the subject of this story.

In Berlin there lived three brothers, among whom there was such hearty friendship and intimacy as is seldom seen. It so happened one day that the youngest of them went out alone in the evening, saying nothing to his brothers, because he was to meet a young woman in another part of town and go walking with her. But before he came to the appointed place, as he made his way thither immersed in pleasant reveries, out of a dark and lonely spot between two houses he heard a gentle, plaintive cry and something that sounded like a death rattle, which he immediately walked toward; for he thought an animal, or perhaps a child, had met with misfortune and lay there waiting for help. Stepping into the darkness of the secluded place, he saw, with horror, that a man lay there in a pool of his own blood. He bent over the man and asked compassionately what had happened, but there was no reply except for weak moaning and sobbing. The injured man had a knife wound in his heart, and a few moments later passed away in the arms of the one who had come to his aid.

The young man did not know what to do next, and since the slain man showed no further sign of life, the youth, dismayed and disconcerted, proceeded with uncertain footsteps to return to the alley. At that very moment, along came two sentries on duty, and while he was considering whether to call out to them for help or walk away in silence, the sentries, observing his terror-stricken condition, approached him. Seeing the blood on his shoes and coat sleeves, they seized him by force, scarcely listening to what he now was beseechingly trying to tell them. They found the dead man close by, the body already cold; and without delay they took the alleged murderer to prison, where he was put in irons and closely guarded.

The next morning, the judge heard his case. The corpse was brought out; and now, in broad daylight, the youth recognized him as a journeyman blacksmith whose companionship he had occasionally enjoyed. But in his prior testimony he had stated that he neither recognized nor knew anything at all about the slain man. Thus, the suspicion that he had stabbed the man grew stronger. And, during the course of the day, witnesses who knew the dead man came forward and testified that formerly the youth had cultivated a friendship with the blacksmith but they had fallen out on account of a young woman. Though there was but little truth in this, there was still a small grain, which the innocent man fearlessly admitted, asserting his innocence and asking, not for mercy, but for justice.

The judge was persuaded that the youth was the murderer, and soon thought he had sufficient evidence to pass judgment and turn him over to the hangman. The more the prisoner disavowed his prior testimony, claiming to know nothing at all, the more guilty he appeared to be.

In the meantime, one of his brothers—the eldest had gone abroad on business the day before—returned home, and waited and looked for the youngest in vain. When he heard that his brother was in prison, accused of committing a murder which he stubbornly denied, he went immediately to see the judge.

"Your Honor," he said, "you have imprisoned an innocent man. Release him. I am the murderer, and I do not want an innocent man to suffer in my place. The blacksmith was my enemy; I had been following him, and last night I met up with him when some private urge brought him to that very corner; then I went after him and plunged the dagger into his heart."

Astonished, the judge listened to this confession and had the brother shackled and closely guarded until such time as the truth should come to light. And so both brothers lay in chains under the same roof, but the youngest knew nothing of what his brother had done for him, and he went on zealously protesting his own innocence.

Two days went by without the discovery of any new evidence, and now the judge was inclined to believe the testimony of the ostensible murderer who had turned himself in. Then the eldest brother returned to Berlin from his business abroad, found no one at home, and learned from the neighbors what had happened to his youngest brother and how his other brother had himself gone before the judge. Then he went out into the night, had the judge awakened, and knelt before him, saying: "Your Honor! Two innocent men are lying in chains suffering for my crime. Neither of my two brothers killed the journeyman blacksmith, but rather it was I who committed the murder. I cannot bear to have others imprisoned in my place, others who have committed no offense whatsoever; and I sorely entreat you to release them and take me, for I am ready to pay for my crime with my life."

Now the judge was even more astonished and knew no other recourse but to take the third brother into custody as well.

Early the next morning, however, when the warder brought the youngest prisoner his bread, he said as he passed it through the door: "Now, I really would like to know the truth as to which of you three really is the monster." No matter how the youngest pleaded and begged, the warder would not tell him anything more; but the youth concluded from these words that his brothers had come to offer their lives in place of his. Then he burst into tears and demanded vehemently to be brought before the judge. As he stood in chains before him, he again began to weep and said: "Oh, your Honor, pardon me for having put you off so long! I thought that no one had seen what I'd done, that no one could prove my guilt. But now I realize that justice will have its way, I can struggle no longer and want to confess that indeed it was I who killed the blacksmith, and it is I who must pay for it with my wretched life."

Then the judge, thinking that he was dreaming, opened his eyes wide in astonishment; his wonder was indescribable, and his heart began to cower in the face of this unusual turn of events. Once again he had the prisoner locked up and put under guard, as he did his two brothers, and for a long time he sat lost in thought. He realized, of course, that only one of the brothers could be the murderer and that the others had offered themselves up to the hangman out of magnanimity and a strange kind of brotherly love.

His meditations came to an end as he understood that the reasoning that generally applied produced no results in this case. Thus, the next day, he left the prisoners in protective custody and went to see the Elector, to whom he related the remarkable story as clearly as possible.

The Elector listened to him with the greatest astonishment, and in the end said: "This is a strange and unusual case! In my heart I believe that none of the three has committed the murder, not even the youngest, whom your sentries apprehended, but rather that all he said in the beginning is the truth. However, since this concerns a crime punishable by death, we cannot simply allow the accused to go free. Thus I will call upon God Himself to pronounce judgment on these three loyal brothers, and to His judgment they must submit."

And so his plan was carried out. It was springtime, and on a bright warm day the three brothers were taken out to a green plot of ground; and each one was given a strong young linden tree to plant. But they were to plant the lindens not with their roots but with their young green crowns in the earth, so that the roots stood out against the sky; and whose sapling would be the first to perish or wither, he would be regarded as the murderer and judged accordingly.

And so each of the brothers carefully dug a hole for his little tree and planted its branches in the earth. Only a short time had passed when all three of the trees began to bud and set new crowns, a sign that all three brothers were innocent. And the lindens quickly grew tall and stood for many hundreds of years in the cemetery of the Hospital of the Holy Ghost in Berlin.

The Man of the Forests

IN THE BEGINNING of the Age of Man, even before the
human race had spread over the face of the earth, there
were the men of the forests. They lived, timid and confined,
in the twilight of the tropical primeval forests, perpetually
in battle with their relatives the apes, while over them
stood the one godhead and the one law that governed
them in all their actions: the Forest. It was their homeland,
refuge, cradle, nest, and grave, and life outside its bound-
aries was unthinkable. Even approaching its borders was
to be avoided, and whosoever—through some strange turn
of Fate—was forced toward them, in hunting or fleeing,
told in fear and trembling of the white Void beyond, where
one could see the fearful Nothingness glistening in the
deadly burning rays of the sun. An old man of the forest,
who decades before had fled from wild beasts beyond the
forest's outermost rim, still lived, blind from that day. He
was now a kind of priest and holy man and was called
mata dalam (he whose eye is turned inward). It was he
who had composed the sacred Song of the Forest, which
was sung whenever there was a great storm, and the forest
people listened to him. That he had seen the sun with
his own eyes and had survived was his glory and the
secret of his power.

(83

The forest people were small and brown and very hairy; their posture was hunched, and they had timid, wild eyes. Like men and like apes, they could walk, and they felt just as secure high in the branches as they did on the ground. As yet they had no knowledge of building houses and huts, but they used various weapons and tools, and they made jewelry. Out of hardwoods they made bows, arrows, lances, and clubs. From bast fiber they made necklaces, hung with dried berries or nuts, and around their necks or in their hair they also wore other objects of value: boars' teeth, tigers' claws, parrots' feathers, the shells of freshwater mussels. Through the middle of the immense forest flowed the great river; the men of the forest, however, dared to walk along its bank only in the darkness of night, and many of them had never seen it. Sometimes the more courageous crept out of the thicket at night, shy and wary, and in the shimmering darkness they would see the elephants bathing, and when they looked up through the overhanging treetops, with terror they beheld the radiant stars hanging in the network of the many-armed mangroves. They had never seen the sun, and it was considered extremely dangerous even to glimpse its reflection in the summer.

In that clan of forest people over which the blind *mata dalam* presided there was also a youth named Kubu; he was leader and spokesman for the young and discontented. Since the *mata dalam* had grown older and more tyrannical, the ranks of the discontented grew. Until now, it had been the blind one's special right to have his food provided for him by the others; they also looked to him for advice, and they sang his Forest Song. But gradually he began to introduce all sorts of burdensome new customs, which, he claimed, the God of the Forest had revealed to him in dreams. But a few young skeptics maintained that the old man was an impostor, who had only his own best interests in mind.

The most recent custom the *mata dalam* had instituted was a celebration of the new moon. Beating on a bark drum, he sat in the center of a circle while the other forest people danced around him in a ring, singing *golo elah* until they dropped, dead-tired, to their knees. At this point, each male had to pierce his left ear with a thorn, and the young women were brought before the priest, who pierced each one's ear with a thorn. Kubu and a few of his companions had avoided this ceremony, and they were set on persuading the girls to offer resistance too.

One time they had a chance to put an end to the priest's power and to triumph over him. The old man was again holding the celebration of the new moon, piercing the left ears of the young females. As he did this, a strong young woman stood up and began to scream terribly; and so it happened that the blind one pierced her eye with the thorn, and blood poured from the eye. Now she screamed so desperately that everyone came running, and when they saw what had happened, they fell into a dazed and angry silence. Exultant now, the boys intervened and Kubu even dared to grab hold of the priest's shoulder. But the old man stood up by his drum and crowed in a scornful voice so ghastly a curse that everyone drew back in fear, and Kubu's own heart froze. No one could understand the precise meaning of the old priest's words, but the manner and sound of his utterance wildly and terribly recalled to them the awesome words of the divine service. And he laid a curse on the youth's eyes, which he commended to the hawk for food; and he cursed the youth's entrails, prophesying that one day they would broil in the sun in the open field. But then the priest, whose power was greater now than at any other time, ordered the young woman to come back to him, and he plunged the thorn through her other eye. And everyone looked on, horrified, and no one dared to breathe.

"You will die Outside," was the curse the old one had put on Kubu, and from then on everyone avoided the youth as one beyond all hope. "Outside"—that meant outside the bounds of their homeland, outside the bounds of the darkening forest! "Outside," that meant terror, scorching sun, and the glowing, fatal Void.

Terrified, Kubu fled, and when he saw everyone who encountered him shrink back, he hid in a hollow tree trunk and admitted defeat. For days and nights he lay there, vacillating between fear of death and defiance, uncertain now whether the people of his clan would come to strike him down or whether the sun itself would break through the forest, besiege and hunt him down, take him captive, and slay him. But neither arrow nor lance, neither sun nor bolt of lightning came to Kubu, nothing came but extreme weariness and the bellowing voice of hunger.

Then Kubu got back on his feet and crawled out of the tree, sober and with a feeling that bordered on disappointment.

"The curse of the priest is powerless," he thought in amazement. Then he went out searching for food, and after he had eaten and could again feel life coursing through his limbs, pride and hatred returned to his soul. He no longer wanted to go back among his people. He wanted to be a loner and an outcast, one whom the people despised, one upon whom the priest—that blind animal—called down impotent curses. He wanted to be alone and to remain alone. But first he would take his revenge.

He went off to think. He contemplated all those things which had ever sowed doubt in his mind, things which appeared to be deceit, and foremost he contemplated the priest's drum and his ceremonies; and the more he thought and the longer he was alone, the more clearly he could see: yes, it was deceit, all of it was nothing but deceit and lying. And since he had already come so far, he thought still further and aimed his now vigilant suspiciousness directly at all that was held to be sacred and true. What, for example, was the truth about the God of the Forest, and the sacred Song of the Forest? Oh, these too were nothing but sheer duplicity! And overcoming a secret terror, he began to sing the Song of the Forest with

(87

scorn and contempt in his voice, twisting all its words, and three times he called upon the God of the Forest, whose name it was forbidden to utter—to all but the priest—on pain of death; yet everything remained peaceful and calm, no storm rent the heavens, no lightning bolt fell from the blue.

For many days and weeks the solitary wandered, with furrowed brow and penetrating gaze. He did something else no one had ever dared: he went to the bank of the river on the night of the full moon. First he looked at the moon's reflection, then at the moon itself; then he gazed into the eyes of all the stars, long and boldly, and nothing untoward befell him. Whole moonlit nights he sat on the riverbank, cherishing his thoughts and reveling in the forbidden delirium of light. Many bold and terrible schemes rose in his soul. The moon is my friend, he thought, and the star is my friend, but the old blind man is my enemy. Thus, the Outside may be better than our Inside, and perhaps the sanctitude of the forest itself is empty talk! And one night, many generations before any human being did, he hit upon a daring and fabulous idea. In all probability, one could bind together some branches with bast fiber, set oneself on them, and float downstream. His eyes sparkled and his heart beat faster, but he did not act on his idea; the river was full of crocodiles.

There was but one way into the future: to go through the forest until he reached its end—if it really had an end—and there to leave it, and put his faith in the glowing Void, the evil Outside. He had to go in search of that

monster the sun and endure it. Because—who could say?
—in the end maybe even the ancient taboo on the sun was
nothing but another lie!

This thought, the last in a bold, feverish sequence, made
Kubu tremble. This was something that no man of the
forest before him had ever dared: voluntarily to leave the
forest and expose himself to the terrifying light of the
sun. And from day to day he went about bearing this
thought in mind. At last he took courage. Trembling, he
crept toward the river in the glare of midday; warily he
neared its glittering bank, and with timid eyes he sought
out the image of the sun in the water. The radiance
pained and dazzled his eyes; he had to close them quickly,
but after a while he dared to open them again, and then one
more time, and he succeeded. It was possible, it was to be
borne; moreover, it made one spirited and brave. Kubu put
his faith in the sun. He loved it, even if it should kill him;
and he hated the old, dark, putrid forest, where the priests
shrilled, and from which he, the young valiant, had been
outlawed and outcast.

Now his resolve had grown ripe, and he plucked the
deed like a sweet fruit. He made a fine, new hammer of
ironwood and equipped it with a very thin, light handle.
Early the next morning, he went after the *mata dalam*,
tracked him down and found him, hit him on the head
with the hammer and watched his soul escape through the
crooked mouth. Kubu laid down his weapon on the old
man's breast, so that people would know how the old man
had met his end; on the hammer's smooth surface, with

the shell of a mussel, he had painstakingly scratched a sign, a circle out of which radiated several straight lines: the image of the sun.

Courageously, he set out on his journey to the distant Outside, and from morning to night he walked in one direction, and at night he slept in the tree branches and continued on his way in the early morning, all day long for several days, crossing over streams and black swamps, and over rising land and mossy banks of stone, the likes of which he had never before seen, and finally upward more steeply, stopped by ravines, farther on into the mountains, and always through the eternal forests, so that in the end he became doubtful and sad, pondering the possibility that perhaps some god really did forbid the creatures of the forest to leave their homeland.

Then one evening, after he had long been climbing and climbing in ever-higher, drier, and thinner air, he came, unexpectedly, to the end. But with the end of the forest came the end of the earth as well; here the forest plummeted down into the emptiness of air, as if here the world had been broken in two. There was nothing to see but a distant, feeble redness, and above, a few stars, for night had already begun to fall.

Kubu sat down at the edge of the world and bound himself fast with vines so as not to fall off. He spent the night crouching in horror and wild agitation, his eyes wide open, and in the first gray of morning he impatiently jumped to his feet and waited, bent over the Void, for day to come.

The Man of the Forests

Lovely yellow strips of light glimmered in the distance, and the sky seemed to tremble in expectation, just as Kubu trembled, never before having seen the coming of day in the broad expanse of the atmosphere. Yellow bundles of light flared up, and on the other side of the monstrous abyss, the sun sprang, huge and red, into the sky. It leapt up out of an endless, gray nothingness, which soon became blue-black: the sea.

Before the trembling man of the forests, the Outside lay unveiled. At his feet, the mountain plunged down into unknowable, smoking depths; opposite him, a craggy mountain chain sprang up, glittering like rosy jewels. To his side, the dark sea lay distant and immense; its coast was white and frothy, and the tiny trees that lined it nodded toward him. And over all this, over these thousand, strange, new, powerful forms, the sun rose and poured a glowing stream of light on the world, which took fire in laughing colors.

Kubu was not able to look the sun in the face. But he saw its light streaming in colorful torrents around the mountains and cliffs and coasts and distant blue isles. And he sank to his knees, bent his face to the earth, bowing down to the gods of this radiant world. Who was he, Kubu?! Only a small, dirty animal who had spent his whole musty life in a darkening bog hole deep in the forest, timid and gloomy, paying homage to obscure gods. But here was the world, and its supreme god was the sun. The long, ignominious dream of his forest life was behind him; now it began—like the sallow image of the dead priest—to be extinguished in his soul. On hands and feet,

Kubu clambered down the steep abyss, toward the light and the sea. And his soul trembled in a fleeting transport of joy with the dreamlike surmise of a bright earth—an earth ruled by the sun, where bright, free beings lived in light, subject to no one but the sun.

The Dream of the Gods

Preliminary Remark

TEN YEARS have now passed since the beginning of the Great War. Among all the memories of that time, there exist in every part of the world numerous instances of presentiments, prophesies, prophetic dreams, and visions which relate to the war. These experiences have resulted in a good deal of humbug, and nothing is further from my intention than to count myself among the ranks of the many clairvoyants and prophets of the war! In August of 1914 I was as shocked and terrified as any man by the course of events. And yet, just like thousands of others, shortly before the onset of the catastrophe, I, too, had a presentiment. At least I had, some eight weeks before war broke out, a very remarkable dream, which I wrote down before the end of June of that year. To be sure, this sketch no longer is an authentic, literally faithful account of the dream; for at that time I made it into a small fiction. But the essential point, the appearance of the God of War and his retinue, was not a conscious invention; rather, it was true to the experience of the dream.

Not as a mere curiosity, but because many people may be inclined to think seriously about it, I present here that sketch from June 1914. [1924]

I WAS ALONE and helpless and saw it grow dark and form-
less everywhere, and searching I ran to find out whither all
brightness had fled. And I saw a new building whose windows were radiant, and over its doors light burned clear as
day, and I went in through a gateway and entered an
illuminated hall. Many people had assembled here and
sat silent and attentive, for they had come to the priests
of knowledge to find consolation and light. On a raised
platform before the people stood one of the priests, a quiet
man dressed in black, with wise, weary eyes, and he spoke
to the large audience in a clear, mild, compellingly serene
voice. But before him on luminous screens were numerous
images of the gods, and now he stepped in front of the
God of War and told how once, in times gone by, this
god had arisen out of the needs and wishes of a people,
who had not yet recognized the unity of all the powers of
the world. No, these people from an earlier time could
only see the particular manifestation, and so they required
and created a particular divinity for the sea, and for dry
land, for the hunt and for war, for the rain and for the
sun. And just so had the God of War arisen, and the
servant of wisdom explained clearly and distinctly where
the first images of that god had been raised, and when the
first sacrifices had been made to him—until later, with the
triumph of knowledge, this god had become superfluous.

With a motion of the priest's hand, the image of the
God of War was extinguished and vanished, and in its
place on the screen rose a picture of the God of Sleep, and
this image, too, was explained—oh, far too quickly, for I

would have liked to hear much more about this benign god. After his image sank out of sight, there appeared in succession the God of Drunkenness, and the God of Joyous Love, and the Goddesses of Agriculture, of the Hunt, and of Domesticity. In its particular form and beauty, each of these divinities flashed like a salutation and reflection from the distant youthful days of humanity. And all were accounted for individually, along with the reasons they had long ago become superfluous. One image after another was extinguished and vanished, and every time this happened, a small and distinct exultation of the spirit, mingled with a feeling of gentle compassion and regret, pulled at our hearts. But a few people laughed continually, clapped their hands, and cried out "Away with it!" whenever another image of a god vanished at the signal of the learned man.

Listening intently, we learned that birth and death, love and envy, hate and anger no longer required special emblems, because, of late, humanity had had enough of all these gods, having recognized that no individual powers or properties resided in either the human soul or the interior of the earth and sea. On the contrary, there was only the great ebb and flow of the one original force, the investigation of whose essence henceforth would be the great task facing the human spirit. In the meantime, whether through the fading of the images, or as the result of other causes unknown to me, the hall had grown more and more dark and dusky, and so I realized that—even here in this temple—no pure and eternal source would illuminate me, and I resolved to flee this house and seek out brighter climes.

But before my resolve had turned to action, I saw the duskiness of the hall grow even murkier, and the people began to feel uneasy, to scream, to crowd and push one another like sheep frightened by a sudden storm, and no one wanted to listen to the wise man's words any longer. A horrible anguish and closeness had settled on the multitude; I heard sighs and groans and watched the frenzied people storm toward the gates. The air was clouded with dust thick as sulfur fumes, it had grown dark as night, but behind the high windows a turbulent incandescence—as of fire—flared muddy red.

My senses left me, I lay on the ground, and countless fugitives trod me with their shoes.

When I came to and raised myself on my bleeding hands, I was all alone in an empty, devastated house, whose crumbling walls split and threatened to crash down on top of me. And I could hear an indistinct din of distant thunder and desolate echoes raging. And through the shattered walls the luminous air, like an agonized, bleeding countenance, pulled away involuntarily from the glowing incandescence. But the suffocating closeness was gone.

As I now crept forth from the ruins of the Temple of Knowledge, I saw half the city in flames and the night sky suffused with pillars of flame and trails of smoke. The dead lay scattered among the debris; it was quiet all about, and I could hear the crackling and blistering of the distant sea of flames, but behind it, out of an even greater distance, I heard a wild and anxious howling, as though all the peoples of the earth raised their voices in one endless scream or sigh.

The world is going under, I thought, and this notion so little surprised me, it seemed as though I had been waiting a long time for just that to happen. But now, from amid the burning and collapsing city, I saw a boy come toward me. His hands were buried in his pockets and he hopped and skipped from one leg to another, resilient and light-hearted. Then he stopped and emitted an ingenious whistle —our signal to one another from Latin School days, and the boy was my friend Gustav, who had shot himself when he was a student. Immediately I too became, like him, a boy of twelve, and the burning city and the distant thunder and the blustering storm of howling voices from all the corners of the world sounded wondrously exquisite to our newly awakened ears. Now everything was good, and the dark nightmare in which I had lived for so many despairing years was gone forever.

Laughing, Gustav showed me a castle with a high tower, and just as he pointed, it all came tumbling down. Never mind if the things perished, no cause for sorrow. Newer and more beautiful things could be built. Thank God Gustav had come back! Now life had meaning again.

An enormous cloud had gathered above the ruins of the splendid buildings, and we stared at it in expectancy and silence; out of this dust cloud a monstrous form broke free, craning its divine head and raising its colossal arms, and it stepped, victorious, into the smoke-filled world. It was the God of War, just as I had seen him in the Temple of Knowledge. But he was alive and gigantic, and his face, lit by flames, smiled proudly in happy, boyish exuberance. And we followed him—our enraptured hearts beating wildly—as if on wings, above the city and the fire, rashly storming away into the broad, fluttering, stormy night.

On a high mountaintop the war god stood exultantly shaking his round shield, and lo—from all the ends of the earth remote gods and goddesses, demons and demi-gods arose and approached him, huge, holy, and splendid. The God of Love came floating, and the God of Sleep came staggering; the Goddess of the Hunt strode slender and severe, and on and on, gods without end. And when, blinded by the nobility of their figures, I cast down my eyes, I saw that I was no longer alone with my cherished friend, but surrounding us on bended knees were a new people, who knelt in the night to the returning gods.

The Painter

A PAINTER by the name of Albert could not in his early years achieve the effects or results he desired with the pictures he painted. He went off by himself and decided to rely entirely on his own judgment. For years he tried to do this. But more and more it was evident that he alone was not enough. He sat working on the portrait of a hero, and while he painted, time and again came the recurrent thoughts: Is it really imperative for you to do what you are doing? Do these pictures really and truly need to be painted? Wouldn't it be just as well for you and for everyone else if you merely spent your time taking walks or drinking wine? What more are you doing with your painting than dulling your nerves a little, forgetting yourself a little, whiling away the time?

These thoughts were not conducive to good work. In time, Albert virtually stopped painting altogether. He went out for walks, he drank wine, he read books, he took trips. But he was not content doing these things either.

Often he had to reconsider those wishes and hopes he had when he initially took up painting. And he remembered what they had been: he had hoped there would emerge a strong and beautiful connection, a current between himself and the world, something powerful and intimate that would perpetually vibrate and make gentle music. In painting heroes and epic landscapes, Albert had sought to appease and express his inner self, so that later —reflected in the appreciative eyes and sound judgment of those who viewed his paintings—it would gratefully shine back at him, invested with new life.

But this had not come to pass. It had become a dream, and even the dream gradually began to weaken and fade away. Wherever Albert roamed, in whatever remote place he sojourned alone, traveling on ships or crossing mountain passes, the dream returned to him more and more frequently, different from before, but just as beautiful, just as powerful, alluring, just as desirable and radiant in the new force of its wishfulness.

How often he had longed for it—to feel a sympathetic vibration between himself and all the things of the world! To feel that his own breath and the breath of the wind and the sea were one and the same, that brotherhood and fellowship, love and intimacy, sound and harmony existed between him and all things!

He no longer wanted to paint pictures that would bring him understanding and love, that would explain, justify, and celebrate him. He no longer thought about heroes and pageantry which—as image and empty smoke—would express and transcribe his own essence. He longed only for the feeling of that vibration, that power current, that secret intimacy, in which he himself would be annihilated and perish, would die and be reborn. Even now this new dream, even now this new, intensified longing made life bearable, brought something like meaning to it, transfigured and redeemed it.

Albert's friends, insofar as he still had some, did not find it easy to understand these visions of his. All they could see was that he kept more and more to himself, that he spoke and smiled more softly and more curiously, that he often disappeared, that he showed no interest in what other people held dear and important—neither politics nor trade, neither shooting matches nor ball games, nor clever discussions about art; in short, he took no part in any of those things in which the others delighted. He had become an eccentric and half crazy. He would go running through the cool, gray winter air, inhaling its colors and scents; he would run after a small child who walked along babbling to himself; he would stare for hours into a pool of green water, or at a flower bed; or he would lose himself—like a reader in his book—in the lines he found in a cross section of a small piece of wood, in a root or a turnip.

People no longer paid him any mind. In those days, he had gone to live in a town in a foreign country and one morning, while walking down a tree-lined boulevard, Albert looked out between the tree trunks and saw a small, sluggish river, a steep, yellow, clayey bank, where bushes and briers had taken root and dustily branched out over fallen rocks and bleak minerals. Then something in him began to sing, he stood still, there in his soul once again were the strains of an ancient song. Clay-yellow and dusty green, or sluggish river and precipitous bank, some kind of relationship between the colors or lines, some kind of tone, a

peculiarity in the random scene was beautiful, unbeliev-
ably beautiful, touching and deeply moving; it spoke to
him, was kindred to him. And he felt the sympathetic
vibration and the most intimate relationship between the
woods and the river, between the river and himself, between the sky, the earth, and the plants; all these things
seemed to be there for the sole purpose of being reflected
as a unity in his eyes and heart, at this hour coming together and bidding welcome. His heart was the place
where river and plant, tree and air could conjoin, bond
together, enhance one another and celebrate a banquet
of love.

When this glorious experience had recurred a few times,
a splendid feeling of joy enveloped the painter, thick and
full as a golden evening or a fragrant garden. He tasted it,
it was sweet and heavy, but he could not long endure it; it
was too rich, it filled him to bursting, it made him agitated,
anxious and frenzied. It was stronger than he, it carried
him away, transported him, and he was afraid of drown-
ing in it. And that was the one thing he did not want. He
wanted to live, he wanted to live an eternity. Never, never
before had he so intensely desired to live as he did now!

As if he had awakened from a spell of delirium, one day
he found himself quiet and alone in a room. Before him
were a box of paints and a small piece of stretched pasteboard—now, after years, he sat down once again to paint.

And so it went. The thought, Why am I doing this? did
not enter his mind. He painted. He did nothing but see and
paint. Either he would go outside and lose himself in the

images of the world, or he would sit in his room and again let the abundance flow off. On his small pieces of pasteboard he painted picture after picture, a rainy sky with willows, a garden wall, a bench in the woods, a highway, or even people and animals and things he had never seen, heroes or angels perhaps, but things which were real and had their own existence, just like walls and forests.

When he returned to the company of men, everyone knew he was painting again. People thought him to be slightly deranged, but they were curious to see his pictures. He did not want to show them to anyone, but people would not leave him in peace. They tormented him and cajoled him. Finally he gave an acquaintance the key to his room, while he himself went on a trip, not wanting to be present when other people looked at his pictures.

The people came, and a great cry went up. A fabulous new painter had been discovered, an eccentric to be sure, but one whom God had favored—or those were the terms used by the critics and connoisseurs.

In the meantime, the painter Albert had ended up in a village and had rented a room at a farm and unpacked his paints and brushes. Again he walked happily through valleys and over mountains, and all he felt and experienced was later mirrored in his paintings.

One day, while sitting over a glass of wine in a tavern, Albert read in the newspaper of the capital how all the world had gone to his home to see his paintings. It was a long, lovely article. Its headline was his name, printed in thick boldface type, and everywhere inflated words of praise oozed from the columns. But the longer he read, the stranger it all seemed to him.

"How marvelously the yellow of the background glows in the picture of the 'Blue Woman'—a new, unprecedentedly bold, bewitching harmony!"

"Wondrous, too, is the plasticity of expression in the 'Still Life with Roses.' —And the series of self-portraits! They may be compared with the finest masterpieces of the art of psychological portraiture!"

Curious, curious, indeed! He could not remember ever having painted a still life with roses, or a blue woman, and never to his knowledge had he painted a self-portrait. And yet he could find no mention of the clay bank or the angel, of the rainy sky, or any of the other paintings which were so dear to him.

Albert returned to the city. Still in traveling clothes, he went to his apartment and found people coming and going. A man sat in the doorway and Albert had to buy a ticket to gain admission.

There were his celebrated paintings. Someone had put labels on them, labels which said all sorts of things Albert knew nothing about at all. For a while he stood contemplating the pictures with their unfamiliar names. He saw that people could give them entirely different names from those he had chosen. He saw that what he had portrayed in "The Garden Wall" appeared to others to be a cloud, and the chasms of his "Stone Landscape" could just as well represent a human face.

In the end, it made little difference. But Albert preferred

to go away again, to travel, and never again return to this city. He went on to paint many more pictures and gave them as many names, and he was happy doing so; but he showed his pictures to no one.

Tale of the Wicker Chair

A YOUNG MAN sat in his lonely garret. He wanted to become a painter, but there were many serious obstacles to be overcome. At first he lived quietly in his garret, growing somewhat older. He had acquired the habit of sitting in front of a small mirror for hours and tentatively sketching his own likeness. He had already filled a whole notebook with these sketches, and with a few of them he was quite content.

"Considering that I have had no formal training," he said to himself, "this sketch has actually come off quite well. And what an interesting crease that is over there by the nose. One can see there's something of the intellectual in me, or at least something like that. All I need to do is extend the corners of the mouth a tiny bit farther down, then it will have such an individual expression—downright melancholy."

But later, after some time had passed, when he looked at the sketches again, he discovered that most of them no longer pleased him at all. This was disagreeable, but he came to the conclusion that he was making progress and that he should make even greater demands on himself.

The young man did not live in the most desirable and intimate relationship with his garret and the things that stood and lay about it; nevertheless, this relationship was not a bad one. He did his things no greater and no lesser injustice than most people do; he scarcely saw them and knew them but poorly.

When a self-portrait again would fall short of the mark, from time to time he would read books, from which he learned how others had fared, other young unknowns who like him had started off from modest beginnings, only later to achieve wide renown. He delighted in reading such books, and in them he read his own future.

And so one day, when again he was somewhat sullen and depressed, he sat at home reading about an extremely famous Dutch painter. This painter had been in the throes of a genuine passion, one might even call it a frenzy, quite completely governed by the impulse to become a good painter. In reading further, he discovered various other things which were not quite applicable to his own case. He read how, during stormy weather, when he could not paint out of doors, the Dutchman steadfastly and passionately had copied every thing, even the lowliest, that came within his field of vision. Just so had he come to paint an old pair of wooden shoes. On another occasion he painted an old crooked chair, a coarse, crude kitchen or peasant chair made of ordinary wood, with a seat of woven straw that was pretty nearly worn to shreds. And he painted this chair—which otherwise would certainly never have been vouchsafed a single human glance—with so much love and fidelity, so much passion and devotion, that the painting had become one of his finest works. The book's author had many candid and moving words to say about the painting of the straw chair.

Here the reader paused for reflection. This was something new for him to attempt. He immediately decided— for he was a young man given to extremely rash decisions —to emulate the example of the great master and try to set his own foot on the path to greatness.

He looked around his attic room and noticed that he had never really taken a good look at the things among which he lived. Nowhere could he find a bandy-legged chair whose seat was of woven straw, nor were there any wooden shoes lying around, and thus for a moment he became dejected and despondent. He felt discouraged again, as he so often did when he read about the lives of great men. All the little signs and hints and marvelous coincidences which had played such a wonderful role in their lives were lacking in his own, and it was useless to expect them. And yet he quickly pulled himself together, realizing that the time was ripe for him to face up to his task and stubbornly pursue this difficult path to fame. He inspected all the objects in his little room and discovered a wicker chair that would serve him well as a model.

With his foot, he pulled the chair a bit closer to him; he sharpened his pencil, put his sketchbook on his knee, and began to sketch. The first few gingerly strokes seemed satisfactorily to indicate the form, and now he began rashly and energetically to ink in the sketch, and with a few more strokes he hastily got down the bold contours. In one corner a deep, triangular shadow enticed him, he accentuated it, and so he went on, until one thing or another would disturb him.

He went on like this for a while, then held the sketch-book at a distance and probingly examined his sketch. He saw that the wicker chair was very badly drawn. Angrily he sketched in a new line, and then he glared furiously at the chair. Something was wrong. This made him very angry.

"You Devil of a chair!" he cried out vehemently. "Never in all my days have I seen such an ill-tempered beast!"

The chair creaked a little and said in an even-tempered voice: "Yes, just look at me! I am as I am, and no more will I change."

The painter kicked the chair with the tips of his toes, and the chair retreated. Now it looked entirely different.

"You stupid idiot of a chair," the young man cried. "Now you look all crooked and lopsided!"

The wicker chair smiled a little and said softly: "That, young man, is what is known as perspective."

At this, the youth sprang to his feet. "Perspective!" he screamed in rage. "Now this rascal of a chair wants to play schoolmaster! Perspective is my concern, not yours, mind you!"

The chair said nothing more. The painter furiously paced up and down, until the angry knocking of a cane from the apartment below sounded against the floorboards. Below him lived an older man, a scholar, who tolerated no noise.

He sat down and again studied his most recent self-portrait. But he did not like it. He saw that in reality he himself was more handsome and more interesting than it was, and this was the simple truth.

Now he wanted to go on reading his book. But there was still more to read about the Dutch straw chair, and this irritated him. The author was making such a lot of fuss about that chair, and after all . . .

The young man looked for his beret and decided to go out for a while. He recalled that for quite some time now painting had struck him as unsatisfactory. It offered nothing but torment and disappointment, and finally, even the best painters in the world could portray only the plain surface of things. This was no calling for a man in love with the depths. And, as he had done on more than one occasion, he gave serious thought to following another inclination, one he had had longer still: to become a writer.

The wicker chair was left alone in the garret. It was sorry that its young master had gone. It had hoped that now, once and for all, a proper relationship would develop between them. It certainly would have liked, now and then, to have said a few words, and it knew that, doubtless, it could pass on quite a lot of valuable information to a young man. But now, unfortunately, nothing would come of it.

Conversation with the Stove

H E INTRODUCED HIMSELF to me, stout, squat, his huge mouth full of fire. His name was Franklin.

"Are you Benjamin Franklin?" I asked.

"No, just Franklin. Francolino. I am an Italian stove, a first-rate invention. Admittedly, I don't heat particularly well, but as an invention, as a product of a highly developed industry—"

"Yes, I'm aware of that. All stoves with fine names heat only reasonably well, and yet they are excellent inventions; many of them are even marvelous feats of industry, as I know from reading their prospectuses. I am exceedingly fond of them, they merit our admiration. But tell me, Franklin, how is it that an Italian stove has an American name? Isn't this a bit odd?"

"No, not really. It is one of the hidden laws, mind you. Cowardly peoples have folk songs glorifying courage. Loveless peoples have plays extolling love. It's the same with us stoves. An Italian stove usually gets an American name, just as a German stove usually gets a Greek name. They are German and in no way do they heat better than I, but they are called Eureka or Phoenix or Hector's Farewell. The name stirs up powerful associations. So, too, have I been named Franklin. I am a stove, but I could just as well be a statesman. I have a big mouth, give off but little heat, spew smoke through a pipe, bear a good name, and stir up powerful associations. That is how I am."

"Certainly," said I, "I hold you in the highest esteem. Since you're an Italian stove, surely one can also roast chestnuts in you?"

"Certainly one can, everyone is free to try. It is a pastime that many people enjoy. Many people also write poems or play chess. Certainly, one can roast chestnuts in me. They will surely burn and no longer be edible, but still it's a way to pass the time. People love nothing quite so much as a pastime, and since I am a work of man, it is my duty to serve him. We do our simple duty, we monuments, we do exactly what is required of us, no more and no less."

"Did you say monuments? Do you think of yourself as a monument?"

"We are all monuments. We products of industry are all monuments to a human faculty or virtue, a faculty which seldom exists in the lower forms of life, and, among its more highly developed forms, is to be found only in human beings."

"Which faculty is that, Mr. Franklin?"

"The sense for the inappropriate. I am, like many of my peers, a monument to this sense. My name is Franklin, I am a stove, I have a big mouth that eats wood, and a big pipe through which warmth finds the quickest means of escape. What's more, and just as important, I have ornaments—lions and other things—and I have a few valves, the opening and closing of which gives a great deal of pleasure. This, too, serves the pastime, just like the valves on a horn, which the hornplayer can open and close as he pleases. It gives him the illusion of doing something significant; and, in the end, he does do something significant."

"Franklin, you are utterly delightful. You're the cleverest stove I've ever seen. But tell me now, are you a stove or are you a monument?"

"You ask so many questions! Surely you know that man is the only living thing that confers meaning on inanimate objects. That's human nature; I serve man, I am one of his works, I'm content to confirm the facts. Man is an idealist, a thinker. For the beast, the oak is an oak, the mountain a mountain, the wind a wind and no heavenly child. For man, however, everything is divine, rife with meaning, everything's a symbol. Everything signifies something else, something entirely different from what it is. Being and appearance remain at odds. It's an old notion, it goes back, I believe, to Plato. A homicide is an act of heroism, a plague is the finger of God, a war is the glorification of God, a cancer of the stomach is evolution. How then could a stove simply be a stove? On the contrary, it is a symbol, it is a monument, it is a harbinger. No doubt it appears to be a stove, and in a certain sense, so it is; but from its simple face the ancient sphinx mysteriously smiles at you. Even the stove is the carrier of an idea, even it is a mouthpiece for the divine essence. That is why people love it, that is why people pay it the respect that is its due. That is why it heats poorly and only in its immediate vicinity. That is why it is called Franklin."

(113

Pictor's Metamorphoses

PICTOR HAD SCARCELY set foot in Paradise when he found himself standing before a tree that had two crowns. In the leaves of one was the face of a man; in the leaves of the other, the face of a woman. Pictor stood in awe of the tree and timidly asked, "Are you the Tree of Life?"

The tree kept silence. Suddenly, coiling itself around the single trunk that joined the tree's two boughs, there appeared a Serpent. And because the Serpent, and not the tree, was about to reply, Pictor turned around and continued on his way. His eyes widened in wonder and delight at all he beheld. Somehow he knew the Source of Life was near.

Soon enough, he came upon another tree, whose two crowns held the sun and the moon. And once again Pictor asked, "Are you the Tree of Life?"

The sun seemed to nod its assent; the moon smiled down at him. All around grew clusters of flowers, strange and wonderful, unlike any Pictor had ever seen. From within the circles of their many-hued petals, bright faces and eyes peered out at him. Some of the flowers nodded on their stems, smiling and laughing like the sun and the

moon. Others were silent, drunken, sunken within themselves, as if drowned in their own perfumes.

And their colors sang to him: this one a deep mauve
lilac song, that one a dark blue lullaby. Oh, what huge
blue eyes this one had, and how much that one resembled
his first love. The scent of another sang in his mother's
voice, made him recall how they'd walked in the gardens
when Pictor was still a little boy. Yet another flower teased
him, stuck out its tongue, long, arched, and red. He bent
down, put his own tongue to it. The taste was wild and
strong, like honey mixed with rosin, and yes, like a
woman's kiss.

Pictor stood alone amid the flowers. Filled with longing
and timid joy, he could feel his heart beating in his chest,
now fast—in anticipation of something he could only surmise; now slow—in time with the rolling waves of the
ocean of desire.

Just then, he saw a bird alight in the grass. The bird's
feathers were ablaze with color, each plume a different
color of the rainbow. And he drew nearer to the bird and
asked, "Most lovely Bird, tell me, where can one find
happiness?"

"Happiness," the bird replied, its golden beak brimming
with laughter, "Happiness, Friend, is in each thing, valley
and mountain, flower and gem."

Even as it spoke these words, the bird began to dance,
ruffling its feathers, flapping its wings, turning its head,
beating its tail on the ground, winking, laughing, spinning

around in a whirl of color. When it came to a standstill, what had been a bird was now a many-colored flower: feathers to petals, claws to roots. The transformation was marvelous. But even as Pictor stood there blinking, it went on changing. Weary of being a flower, it pulled up its roots, set its anthers and filaments in motion. On petal-thin wings it slowly rose aloft and floated in mid-air, a weightless, shimmering butterfly. Pictor could scarcely believe his eyes.

And the new butterfly, the radiant bird-flower-butterfly, flew in circles around and around Pictor. More and more amazed, Pictor watched the sunlight glint off its wings. Soon it let itself glide down to the earth gently as a snowflake. There it rested on the ground, close by Pictor's feet. The luminous wings trembled as it changed once again. It became a gemstone, out of whose facets a red light streamed.

But even as it lay there, radiant red in the dark green grass, the precious stone shrank smaller and smaller. As if its homeland, the center of the earth, called to it, the gem threatened to be swallowed up. Just as it was about to vanish, scarcely aware of what he was doing, Pictor reached for the stone, picked it up, and clasped it firmly in his hands. Gazing into it, transfixed by its magical light, Pictor could feel its red rays penetrate his heart, warming it with a radiance that promised eternal bliss.

Just then, slithering down from the bough of a withered tree, the Serpent hissed into Pictor's ear, "This crystal can change you into anything you want to be. Quickly tell it your wish, before it is too late. Swiftly, speak your command, before the stone vanishes."

Without stopping to think, afraid of losing this one chance for happiness, Pictor rashly uttered his secret word to the stone, and was as soon transformed into a tree. Pictor had always wished to become a tree, because trees seemed so serene, so strong and dignified.

He felt himself strike root in the earth, felt his arms branch up into the sky, felt new limbs growing from his trunk, and from the limbs he felt new leaves sprout. Pictor was content. His thirsty roots drank deep in the earth. His leafy crown, so near to the clouds, rustled in the breeze. Birds nested in his branches, insects lived in his bark, hedgehogs and hares took shelter at his feet. For many years, he was happy. A long time passed before he felt something amiss; his happiness was incomplete. Slowly he learned to see with the eyes of a tree. Finally he could see, and grew sad.

Rooted to the spot, Pictor saw the other creatures in Paradise continually transform themselves. Flowers would turn into precious stones or fly away as dazzling hummingbirds. Trees that had stood beside him suddenly were gone: one turned into a running brook, another became a crocodile; still a third turned into a fish—full of life, it swam away joyfully. Elephants became massive rocks; giraffes became long-stemmed flowers. While all creation flowed into one magical stream of endless metamorphosis, Pictor could only look on.

He alone could not change. Once he knew this, all his

happiness vanished. He began to grow old, taking on that tired, haggard look one can observe in many old trees. Not only in trees, but in horses, in birds, in human beings, in all life forms that no longer possess the gift of transformation. As time passes, they deteriorate and decline, their beauty is gone. To the end of their days, they know nothing but sorrow.

Time passed as before, until one day a young girl lost her way in Paradise. She had blond hair; she wore a blue dress. She sang happy songs; dancing, she wended her way among the trees. Carefree, the girl had never thought of wishing for the gift of transformation. Many of the creatures in Paradise took a keen interest in her. Animals smiled at her; bushes stretched their branches out to touch her; many of the trees tossed fruits, nuts, or flowers her way. But she paid them no mind.

The moment Pictor caught sight of her, he felt an intense longing, a firm resolve to recover his lost happiness. It was as if an inner voice, the voice of his own red blood commanded him to take hold of himself, to concentrate, to remember all the years of his life. And he obeyed the voice and became lost in thought, and his mind's eye summoned up images from his past, even from his distant past when he was a man on his way to Paradise. But most clearly he remembered the moment when he had held the magical stone in his hands, when every metamorphosis was open to him, when life had glowed in him more intensely than ever before. Then he remembered the laughing bird and the tree that was both the sun and the moon. And he began to understand all he had lost. The Serpent's advice had been treacherous.

Hearing a loud rustling in Pictor's leaves, the girl turned her gaze on the tree. She looked up at its crown, and felt strange new feelings, desires, and dreams welling up in her heart. What was this unknown force that made her sit down in the shade of the tree? To her, the tree seemed lonely and sad, and yet beautiful, touching, and noble in its mute sorrow. The song of its gently swaying crown held her captive. Leaning against its rough trunk, she could feel the tree shudder deep inside itself, and she felt the same passionate tremor in her own heart. Clouds flew across the sky of her soul, heavy tears fell from her eyes. Her heart hurt her so, beat so hard, she felt it would burst out of her bosom. Why did it want to cleave to him, melt into him, the beautiful loner?

Pictor, too, longed to become one with the girl. And so he gathered in all his life forces, focused them, directed them toward her. Even his roots trembled with the effort. And now he realized how blind he had been, how foolish, how little he had understood life's secret. That deceitful, that treacherous Serpent had had but one wish: to lock Pictor up inside a tree forever. And it was in an entirely different light—albeit tinged with sorrow—that he now saw the image of the tree that was Man and Wife together.

Just then, in an arc, a bird came flying, a bird red and green; lovely, daring, nearer it came. The girl saw it fly, saw something fall from its beak, something that shone blood-red, red as embers; and it fell in the green green grass, so promising; its deep red radiance called to her, courted her, sang out loud. The girl stooped down, picked up the bright red stone. Ruby-garnet-crystal gem, wherever it is, no darkness can come.

The moment the girl held the magical stone in her white hands, the single wish that filled her heart was answered. In a moment of rapture she became one with the tree, transformed as a strong, new bough that grew out of its trunk, higher and higher into the heavens.

Now everything was splendid, the world was in order. In that single moment Paradise had been found. The tired old tree named Pictor was no more. Now he sang out his new name: Pictoria, he sang out loud and clear: Pictoria, Victoria.

Out of a half he had become a whole. Fulfilled, complete, he had attained the true, eternal transformation. The stream of continuing creation flowed through his blood, and he could go on changing forever and ever.

He became deer, he became fish, he became human and Serpent, cloud and bird. In each new shape he was whole, was a pair, held moon and sun, man and wife inside him. He flowed as a twin river through the lands, shone as a double star in the firmament.

The Tourist City in the South

ONE OF THE CLEVEREST and most lucrative under-takings of the modern spirit, the founding and establishment of the Tourist City in the South, rests on an ingenious synthesis—a synthesis that could only have been conceived by the most penetrating psychologists of the mentality of city dwellers, if one does not want to see this as a direct emanation of the soul of the city itself, as its dream made real. For the city realizes, in ideal perfection, all the wishes and hopes the average city dweller could possibly hold out for his vacation and his enjoyment of the great outdoors. As we all know, the city dweller revels in nothing so much as nature, idyllic scenes, peace, and beauty. But, as we know only too well, all these lovely things his heart covets—and in which, until quite recently, the earth was still abundant—are indigestible and intolerable to him. Now that he's got the idea of nature in his head, there has been created for him—just like decaffeinated coffee and nicotine-free cigars—a nature-free, no-risk, hygienic, de-natured nature. Moreover, the supreme rule of the modern industry of applied arts has been strictly enforced: the requirement of absolute "authenticity." And the modern arts trade is right to stress this requirement, one unknown in earlier times, when indeed every sheep was genuine and gave genuine wool, every cow was genuine and gave genuine milk, back in the days before the invention of artificial sheep and cows. Shortly after they had been invented, and had virtually driven out the authentic ones, the ideal of authenticity was born. Gone are the days when naïve princes built for their own enjoyment artificial ruins, a copy of the Hermitage, a small sham Switzerland, or an imitation Posilipo in this or that small German valley. The absurd thought of wanting to simulate for the urban connoisseur something like Italy in the vicinity of London, Switzerland near Chemnitz, or Sicily on Lake Constance lies far from the minds of today's entrepreneurs. The nature substitute that today's city dweller demands must be unconditionally genuine, genuine as the silver on his table, genuine as the pearls around his wife's neck, and genuine as the love for his countrymen and his republic which he cherishes in his bosom.

Making all this real was not easy. For spring and fall, the affluent city dweller demands a South that accords with his own preconceptions and needs, an authentic South replete with palm trees and lemons, blue lakes and picturesque villages; actually, all this was easy enough to achieve. However, that city dweller further demands society, he wants hygiene and cleanliness, a metropolitan atmosphere, music, technology, elegance; he expects his nature to be utterly subjugated and transformed by man, a nature that, to be sure, provides him with any number of alluring enticements, but one which is also tractable and demands nothing of him, one in which he can make himself comfortably at home with all his metropolitan habits and pretensions. Now, because Nature is the most implacable force we know, the fulfillment of such demands would seem virtually impossible; but, as we know, for human ingenuity, nothing is impossible. The dream has come true.

Of course, the Tourist City in the South could not be produced in only one unique specimen. Thirty or forty of these ideal cities were made; they have sprung up at each and every suitable site. And if I attempt to describe one of these cities, of course I won't have any one in particular in mind; it shall remain nameless—like a Ford, it is just one off the line, one of many.

Enclosed by a long, gently curved, reinforced embankment, lies a lake of blue water with quick little waves, at whose rim the enjoyment of nature takes place. Along the shore float numerous little rowboats with colorfully striped awnings and varicolored pennons, elegant, fine boats with neat little cushions, spotless as operating tables. Their owners walk up and down the quay, incessantly offering to charter out their sailing vessels to all passersby. These men are dressed like sailors, they go bare-chested and their bare arms are brown; they speak genuine Italian; nonetheless, they are capable of giving information in every other conceivable language; southern eyes aglow, they smoke long, thin cigars and look quite picturesque.

Along the shore the boats are docked; along the rim of the lake runs the esplanade, a two-lane road. The lakeward lane, under neatly pruned trees, is reserved for

pedestrians; the inland lane is a dazzling, hot thorough-
fare, crowded with hotel buses, autos, tramways, and
vehicles of every description. Fronting on this road is the
Tourist City, which has one dimension fewer than other
cities; it extends in height and width only, but not in depth.
It consists of a thick, tight girdle of proud hotels. But
behind this belt of hotels there's an attraction not to be
missed: the genuine South. There, for all to see, stands an
old Italian town, in whose narrow, strong-smelling marketplace vegetables, poultry, and fish are sold, where barefoot
children play kickball with tin cans, and mothers—their
hair flying—bellow out in powerful voices the euphonious
classical names of their children. Here it smells of salami,
of wine, of the latrine, of tobacco, of manual toil; here
jovial men in shirtsleeves stand in the open doorways of
their shops; shoemakers sit in the street pounding leather,
all very genuine and very gay and original—on this set
the first act of an opera could begin at any time. Here one
can watch the intensely curious tourists make discoveries,
and frequently one can hear the knowing pronouncements
of the educated on the soul of the natives. Ice-cream
venders convey small rattling carts through the narrow
streets and bellow out the names of their sweets; here
and there in a courtyard or a small square a hand organ
begins to play. Each day the tourist spends an hour or two
in this small, dirty, and interesting town, buying picture
postcards and items of woven straw, trying to speak
Italian, garnering his impressions of the South. Here, too,
a lot of picture taking goes on.

The Tourist City in the South

Still farther in the distance, behind the Old Town, lies the countryside with its villages and meadows, its vineyards and forests. There Nature is just as she always was —crude and untamed; but the tourists take little interest in it, because when, from time to time, they drive their automobiles through this thing called Nature, the meadows and villages at the edge of the highway look precisely as dusty and hostile as those everywhere else.

Soon the tourist returns once again from his excursion to the Ideal City. Its big, many-storied hotels are under the management of astute directors with well-trained, courteous, and attentive staffs. Lovely steamers ply the waters of the lake, and elegant vehicles travel the highway. Every footstep alights on asphalt and cement, everywhere you turn it is freshly swept and sprayed, everywhere trinkets and refreshments are for sale. The former President of France is staying at the Hotel Bristol, and the German Chancellor is at the Park Hotel. In elegant cafés one meets one's friends from Berlin, Frankfurt, and Munich, reads the newspapers from one's hometown; coming in out of the old, operettalike Italian town, once again one breathes in the good, solid air of one's homeland, of the metropolis; one presses freshly washed hands, people invite one another to take refreshments, from time to time they make phone calls to their native places of business; trim and stimulated, they move among well-dressed, cheerful people. On the hotel balconies, behind the balustrades and the oleander trees, famous poets sit and fix their pensive gazes on the mirror of the lake; from time to time they receive representatives of the press, and soon one learns about each master's work in progress. In a fine little restaurant one sees the most popular actress of one's native metropolis; she's wearing a gown that is like a dream and she's feeding dessert to her Pekinese. And in the evenings, when she opens her window—in Room 178 of the Palace Hotel—and sees the endless row of shimmering lights that range along the shore and dreamily disappear on the far side of the bay, even she is charmed by the natural scene and is often almost moved to say her prayers.

Mellow and contented, one walks along the esplanade; the Müllers from Darmstadt are there, too, and one hears that tomorrow an Italian tenor—the only one worth listening to since Caruso—will give a recital in the casino. Toward evening, one sees the little steamers returning, inspects those who disembark, again finds acquaintances, lingers awhile in front of a shop window full of old furniture and embroidery; then it gets chilly and it is now time to return to the hotel. Behind the walls of concrete and glass, the dining room sparkles with porcelain, glass, and silver; later in the evening, a little ball will be held here. But the music's already begun; scarcely has one finished making one's evening toilette when one is welcomed by sweet and lulling sounds.

Outside the hotel, planted between the concrete walls are thick, multicolored beds of constantly blossoming flowers: camelias and rhododendrons. Their splendor gradually fades away as evening arrives. Tall palm trees surround them. All this is genuine. And the cool blue globes of the plump hydrangeas are in full bloom. Tomorrow there will be a big tour group going to ——aggio; everyone is looking forward to it. And if one has erred in choosing ——aggio over ——iggio or ——ino perhaps, no matter; because at any of these places one will find the identical Ideal City, the selfsame lake, the quay, the same picturesque and droll Old Town, and the same fine hotels with their high glass walls, behind which the palm trees observe us while we dine, the same good soft music; in sum, all that suits the city dweller when he wants to live in style.

Among the Massagetae

HOWEVER MUCH my native land, supposing that I had one, might doubtless surpass every other country on this earth in its amenities and splendid appointments, not long ago I felt the urge to go traveling again, and I made a trip to the distant land of the Massagetae, where I had not been since the invention of gunpowder. I had a hankering to learn how much these widely celebrated and brave people, whose warriors long ago had vanquished the great Cyrus, had changed since my last visit, and how much they might have adapted to the ways of present-day society.

And indeed my estimation of the valiant Massagetae was by no means too high. Like all countries which have ambitions of being counted among the more advanced, that of the Massagetae nowadays sends a reporter to meet each foreigner who approaches its frontier. Except, of course, when they are venerable and distinguished foreigners; for to them, it goes without saying, far greater honor is shown, to each according to his rank. If they are boxers or soccer champions, they are welcomed by the Minister of Hygiene; if they are competitive swimmers, by the Minister of Cultural Affairs; and if they hold world's records, by the President of the Republic or one of his deputies. Now in my case I was spared having these attentions heaped upon me; I was a man of letters, and thus an ordinary journalist came to meet me at the border, a pleasant young man with a handsome figure, and he requested, before I set foot in his country, that I honor him with a short statement about my philosophy of life, and especially on my views of the Massagetae. It seems this charming custom had also been introduced since my last visit.

"My good sir," I said, "allow me, for I have but an imperfect command of your splendid language, to confine myself only to the most essential observations. My philosophy at any given time is obviously that of the country in which I am traveling. Now, my knowledge of your widely renowned country and people stems from the best and most venerable source imaginable; namely, from the book *Clio* by the great Herodotus. Filled with deep admiration for the valor of her powerful army and for the glorious memory of your heroic Queen Tomyris herself, I have already had the honor of paying a visit to your country on a prior occasion, and now at last I would like to renew my acquaintance."

"Very much obliged," the Massagetes replied, somewhat darkly. "Your name is not unknown to us. Our Ministry of Propaganda conscientiously follows all statements about us that appear in the foreign press, and so it has not escaped our notice that you are the author of some thirty lines about Massagetic habits and customs, which you published in a newspaper. It would be an honor for me to accompany you on your present journey through our land, and to see that you have a chance to observe just how much many of our customs have changed since you were here last."

His somewhat darker tone warned me that my earlier utterances about the Massagetae, whom I nonetheless continued to hold in the highest esteem, had by no means been met with unreserved approbation here in this country. For a moment I considered turning back, remembering how Queen Tomyris had thrust the severed head of the great Cyrus in a skin filled with human blood, along with other fiery manifestations of this lively national spirit. But, after all, I had my passport and my visa, and the days of Tomyris were long gone.

"Pardon me," my guide said now in a somewhat friendlier tone, "if I must first insist on putting your faith to the test. Not that there's even the slightest suspicion of your motives, even though you have visited our country once before. No, only for formality's sake, and because you have, somewhat one-sidedly, called upon Herodotus alone. As you know, in the days of that highly talented Ionian, we did not yet have ministries of propaganda or culture, and so his somewhat negligent statements about our country were allowed to pass. We can no longer allow, however, a present-day author to rely exclusively upon the testimony of Herodotus. —And thus, my esteemed colleague, tell me in a few words your opinion of and feelings for the Massagetae."

I gave a little sigh. I could see that this young man was

not inclined to make things easy for me; he stood on formalities. All right then, formalities it would be. I began: "Obviously, I am well aware that the Massagetae are not only the oldest and most pious, most cultured, and at the same time the bravest people on earth, that their invincible armies are the largest, their fleet the greatest, their character at once the most inflexible and the most amiable, their women the most beautiful, their schools and public buildings the most exemplary in the world, but also that in all the world they possess in the highest degree that virtue which is so highly esteemed and so sorely lacking in many other great peoples: namely, although conscious of their own superiority, they are charitable toward and considerate of foreigners, not expecting each and every poor stranger—coming from an inferior country—to have himself attained the heights of Massagetic perfection. And I shall not fail to make mention of this, in strict accordance with the facts, in my report to my homeland."

"Very good," my companion said charitably. "Indeed you have, in your enumeration of our virtues, hit the nail, or more precisely, the nails, on the head. I see that you are better informed than you initially appeared to be, and from the bottom of my faithful Massagetic heart, I freely and openly welcome you to our lovely country. To be sure, a few gaps in your knowledge of us require some filling in. In particular, it struck me that in mentioning our great accomplishments, you neglected two critical areas of achievement: namely, Sports and Christianity. It was a Massagetes, my good man, who set the international world's record—at 11,098—in hopping backwards while blindfolded."

"Indeed," I smiled politely, "how could I possibly have neglected that! But you also mentioned Christianity as a field in which your people have set records. May I ask you to enlighten me on that score?"

"Well now," the young man said, "I just wanted to point out that it would be gratifying to us, if in writing about your trip, you would add one or two friendly superlatives on this account. For example, in a town on the Araxes we have an old priest who in his lifetime has said no fewer than 63,000 masses, and in another town there is a famous modern church in which everything is made of cement, native cement at that: walls, tower, floors, pillars, altars, roof, baptismal font, pulpit, etc., everything down to the last candlestick, down to the collection plates."

Well, I thought, you probably even have a cement minister standing in a cement pulpit. But I held my tongue.

"Let me be frank with you," my guide went on. "We have an interest in promoting as strongly as possible our image as Christians. Although our nation adopted the Christian religion centuries ago, and although there is no longer any trace of the former gods and cults of the Massagetae, there is still a small, all-too-ardent faction in our country bent on reintroducing the gods from the days of the Persian King Cyrus and Queen Tomyris. This is purely the whim of a few fanatics, mind you, but naturally the foreign press in our neighboring countries seizes upon this ridiculous matter and draws connections between it and the reorganization of our military. We are suspected of wanting to abolish Christianity in our country, so that in the next war, what few restraints remain on the use of weapons of total destruction can more readily be relinquished. This is the reason an emphasis on the Christian nature of our land would be gratifying to us. Of course, nothing is further from our minds than wanting to influence your objective report in the slightest way, and yet for all that, I can tell you in all confidence that your readiness to write some few words on our Christianity could result in a personal invitation from the Chancellor of the Republic. I say this only as an aside."

"I will think the matter over," I said. "Actually, Christianity is not my area of expertise. —But now I would be very happy once again to see the splendid monument that your ancestors erected to the heroic Spargapises."

"Spargapises?" my colleague mumbled. "Now, who would that be?"

"Why, the brave son of Tomyris, who could not bear the disgrace of having been deceived by Cyrus, and who took his own life in prison."

"Oh yes, of course," my companion cried, "I see you keep coming back to Herodotus. Yes, this monument was indeed said to have been very beautiful. It has vanished from the face of the earth in a strange manner. Just listen! We have, as you well know, an insatiable interest in science, especially in archaeological research; and when it comes to the number of square meters excavated or tunneled under for the purposes of research, our country ranks third or fourth in the world. These prodigious excavations, predominantly for prehistoric deposits, were also being carried on in the vicinity of that monument from Tomyris times, and precisely because that terrain promised to yield up great treasures—namely, a deposit of Massagetic mammoth bones—an attempt was made to dig under the monument to a certain depth. And while this was going on, the monument fell over and was destroyed! Fragments of it, however, should still be on display in the Museum Massageticum."

He took me to a car that was standing ready, and engaged in lively conversation, we drove toward the interior of the country.

King Yu

A STORY FROM OLD CHINA

I N THE HISTORY of old China, there are but few examples of regents and statesmen whose downfall came about through the influence of a woman or a romantic involvement. One of these rare examples, and a very remarkable one, is that of King Yu of Dschou and his wife Bau Si.

The kingdom of Dschou abutted, in the west, on the provinces of Mongolian barbarians; its capital, Fong, was situated in the midst of insecure territory, which from time to time was prey to the raids and surprise attacks of those barbarian tribes. Thus, consideration had to be given to the best possible means of strengthening the border defenses, and especially to the better protection of the capital.

By no means a bad statesman, and one who knew when to heed the good advice of his counselors, King Yu, as the history books tell us, was able to compensate for the drawbacks of his border with ingenious devices; but as the history books also tell us, all these ingenious and admirable contrivances eventually came to naught, owing to the capriciousness of a pretty woman.

That same king, with the assistance of all the princes who owed him fealty, created a fortification along the western frontier, and this, like all political constructs, had two dimensions: to wit, one part moral and the other mechanical. The moral component of the agreement between the king and his princes was a loyalty oath which bound the princes and their officials to dispatch themselves and their soldiers to the king's residence to aid him at the very first sign of distress. The mechanical component, which the king devised, consisted in an elaborate system of watchtowers, built along the western frontier. A guard would be posted day and night in each of the towers, which were furnished with huge drums. Now, should an enemy raid occur anywhere along the border, drumbeats would sound in the nearest tower, and from tower to tower the drum signal would fly with utmost speed throughout the land.

For a long time King Yu was occupied with this clever and meritorious project; he conferred with his princes, heard the reports of the master builders, arranged to have the sentries thoroughly trained. But he had a favorite wife by the name of Bau Si, a beautiful woman who knew how to exert more influence over the heart and mind of the king than is good for a ruler or his realm. Like her lord, Bau Si followed the construction works at the frontier with intense curiosity and interest, just as a lively, clever girl sometimes will look on with eager admiration at boys playing their games. In order to make the matter of the border defenses clear to her, one of the master builders made a fine model of painted and fired clay for Bau Si. There in miniature were the border and the system of towers, and in each of the dainty little clay towers stood an infinitely small clay guard, and a tiny bell hung in place of each drum. This charming toy gave the king's wife infinite pleasure; when she happened, now and then, to be in a bad mood, her maidservants would suggest they play "Barbarian Invasion." Then they would set up all the little towers, pull on the strings of the miniature bells, and soon would grow thoroughly amused and exuberant.

It was a great day in the king's life when at last the construction was complete, the drums installed, and their attendants trained to perfection. And now, on a day previously deemed to be auspicious, the new border defenses were put to the test. Proud of his accomplishment, the king was greatly excited; his court officers stood ready to offer congratulations, but more than anyone, the lovely Bau Si was expectant and excited and could scarcely wait for all the preliminary ceremonies and invocations to be over.

At last, things reached the point where the game of towers and drumbeats, in which the king's wife had so often delighted, would be played out in real life. She could scarcely keep herself from intervening in the game and giving orders—so great was her excitement. With a serious look on his face, the king gave her a sign and she managed to control herself. The hour had come; now the game of "Barbarian Invasion" would be played with real, full-sized towers and drums and people, to see if everything would function properly. The king gave the signal, the head court

official passed the order on to the captain of the cavalry;
the captain rode to the first watchtower and gave the order
to sound the drum. The drum boomed forcefully, and its
solemn and gripping tone sounded in every ear. Bau Si
had grown pale with excitement and began to tremble.
Mightily the great war drum sang its harsh earthshaking
song, a song full of warning and menace, full of the
future, of war and misery, of fear and destruction. Everyone listened to it in awe. Now it began to fade, and the
answer came from the next tower, distant and weak and
rapidly dying away, until nothing more was heard, and
after a while the solemn silence was broken, people began
to talk again, to move about and amuse themselves.

In the meantime, the deep, menacing sound of the drum
ran from the second tower to the third, to the tenth, and
to the thirtieth tower, and as soon as they heard it, every
soldier, under strict orders, armed and with his knapsack
filled with provisions, immediately had to proceed to the
rendezvous; every captain and colonel, without losing a
moment's time, had to prepare to march and in all haste
had to send certain orders, as previously determined, to the
interior of the country. Everywhere within earshot of the
sound of the drum, work and meals, games and sleep
were interrupted and replaced by packing, saddling, as-
sembling, marching and riding. As quickly as possible, and
from all the neighboring districts, troops hurried on their
way to the residence Fong.

In Fong, in the middle of the court, the intense emotion
and suspense which, at the sounding of the terrible drum,

had seized every heart had soon subsided. People strolled in the gardens of the residence, stimulated and chatting; the whole city had a holiday, and in less than three hours, large and small cavalcades approached from two sides, and from one hour to the next, new ones arrived. This went on all day and for the whole of the following two days, during which time the king, the officials, and the officers were seized by an ever-increasing enthusiasm. The king was piled high with honors and congratulations, the master builders were given a banquet, and the drummer from Tower I, who had been first to beat the drum, was garlanded, carried through the streets, and given presents by all the people.

Utterly enraptured, as if intoxicated, however, was Bau Si, the king's wife. More glorious than she could ever have imagined, her little game of towers and bells had become real. Enveloped in the broad, vast sound wave the drum produced, the command was magical, and it disappeared into the empty land. And alive, large as life, enormously its issue came streaming back out of the distance; out of the heart-gripping howl of that drum an army had grown, a well-equipped army of hundreds and thousands, who came in a steady stream, in a continuous hurrying motion; archers, light and heavy cavalry, lancers came riding and marching from the horizon, and with increasing turmoil they gradually filled all the space surrounding the city, where they were met and shown their posts, where they were greeted and shown hospitality, where they camped, pitched their tents, and lit their fires. Day and night it went on; like ghosts in a fairy tale, they emerged from the gray ground, distant, minute, veiled in small dust clouds, so that here at last, right before the eyes of the court and the enraptured Bau Si, they stood in formation, overwhelmingly real.

King Yu was well satisfied, and especially so with his enraptured favorite wife; like a flower she beamed with joy, and never before had she looked so beautiful to him. But all holidays must come to an end. Even this great holiday had to fade and yield to the everyday: no more miracles took place, no fairy-tale dreams came true. To idle and moody people, such disappointment is unbearable. A few weeks after the holiday. Bau Si had lost all her good humor. Once she had tasted the big game, the smaller game with the miniature clay towers and the tiny bells with their strings had become vapid. Oh, how intoxicating it had been! And now everything lay ready for a repetition of the rapturous game: there stood the towers and there hung the drums, the soldiers were at their posts and the drummers were in uniform, all waiting, all poised for the great command, and all this was dead and useless as long as no order came!

Bau Si lost her laughter, she lost her radiant disposition; and deprived of his most beloved playmate, of his evening consolation, the king grew sullen. He had to give her more and more extravagant gifts in order to bring a smile to her lips. Now would have been the time to acknowledge the situation and to sacrifice this tender affection on the altar of his duty. But Yu was weak. To see Bau Si laugh again seemed more important to him than anything else in the world.

So he yielded to her temptation—slowly and under protest, but he yielded. Bau Si brought him to the point where he became oblivious of his duty. Succumbing to her entreaties, repeated for the thousandth time, he fulfilled the single great wish of her heart: he acquiesced in giving the signal to the border guards, as if the enemy were in sight. Immediately the deep, agitating voice of the war drum sounded. But this time the king found it terrifying, and even Bau Si was frightened by the sound. But then the whole charming game was reenacted: at the edge of the world little clouds of dust suddenly appeared, the troops came riding and marching, for three whole days the generals bowed, the soldiers pitched their tents. Bau Si was blissful, her laugh was radiant. But these were difficult hours for King Yu. He had to confess that the enemy had not attacked, that everything was peaceful and calm. He tried his best to justify the false alarm, explaining it away as a salutary exercise. He was not contradicted, people bowed and accepted his excuses. But there was talk among the officers; they had been dealt a treacherous blow by the king, he had alarmed the whole border and set everything in motion, all those thousands of people, for the sole purpose of obliging his mistress. And the majority of the officers agreed that never again would they respond to such a command. In the meantime, the king took great pains to appease the disgruntled troops by seeing that they were entertained in a grand fashion. And so Bau Si had attained her goal.

But even before she had time to fall into another one of her bad moods and could again repeat the unscrupulous game, both Bau Si and the king got their punishment. Perhaps by chance, and perhaps because they had gotten wind of this story, one day the barbarians in the west came swarming over the frontier. Instantly the towers gave their signals, the deep drum sound cried its urgent warning and ran even to the farthest border. But this excellent toy, whose mechanism was so greatly to be admired, now appeared to be shattered—certainly the drums sounded, but this time they failed utterly to resound in the hearts of the soldiers and officers of the country. They did not follow the drum, and in vain the king and Bau Si looked out all around them; no dust clouds were rising, no small gray platoons came creeping, no one at all came to the aid of the king.

With what few troops he had on hand, the king hastened toward the barbarians. But these came in great numbers; they killed the king's troops, captured the residence Fong, destroyed the palace and the towers. King Yu lost his kingdom and his life, and things did not go otherwise for his favorite wife, Bau Si, of whose pernicious laugh the history books still tell us today.

Fong was destroyed, the game had been played in earnest. No more would the drums sound, King Yu was no more, and no more was the laughing Bau Si. Yu's successor, King Ping, found no alternative but to abandon Fong and remove his capital far to the east; to insure the future security of his dominion, he had to enter into alliances with the neighboring princes and buy them off by surrendering to them vast tracts of land.

Bird

A FAIRY TALE

B IRD LIVED, in times gone by, within the environs of
Montagsdorf. His coloration was not especially
bright, nor was his song distinctly beautiful, and he was
neither large nor imposing; no, those who have seen him
with their own eyes call him small, even puny. He was
not a lovely bird, but he had in him some measure of the
singular and the sublime, something which all animals
and creatures have and which is not a function of genus
or species. Neither hawk nor fowl, titmouse nor woodpecker nor finch—no others were like him; he was one of
a kind. And people had known about him from time immemorial, from the beginnings of recorded time. And even
if the only people who really knew him were those from
the environs of Montagsdorf, neighbors far and wide had
heard of him; and the inhabitants of Montagsdorf, like all
people who have something special of their very own, were
occasionally teased about him. "The people of Montagsdorf," so it was said, "even have their own bird." From
Careno to Morbio and beyond, people knew of him and
told stories about him. But as is so often the case, only in
more recent times—to be precise, only since his disap-

pearance—have people tried to obtain exact and reliable information about him. Many foreigners came to Montagsdorf to inquire about Bird, and many a native of Montagsdorf allowed himself to be interrogated over a glass of wine, until he finally confessed that he himself never had seen the bird. But if he had never seen Bird himself, then at least he still knew someone who had seen Bird one or more times, and who told stories about him. All this was now being investigated and recorded, and it was strange to see how much these various accounts disagreed with one another, concerning not only Bird's appearance, voice, and manner of flight, but also his habits and dealings with human beings.

In earlier times, sightings of Bird are said to have been more frequent, and whoever encountered Bird always felt joy; each time it was an event, a stroke of luck, a small adventure, just as for nature lovers it is a little event and a piece of luck when now and then they catch sight of a fox or a cuckoo and have a chance to observe it. For in that moment it seems that either the creature loses its fear of the frightful human race, or else the human himself is drawn back into a state of primitive innocence. There were those who did not think very highly of Bird, just as there are those who belittle the discovery of one of the first gentians, or an encounter with a wily old serpent; but there were others who loved him dearly, and for each of them it was a joy and a distinction to encounter him. Once in a great while one heard the opinion expressed that Bird may formerly have been dangerous or perhaps sinister: whoever looked at him would be upset for a time and would have many disturbing dreams at night and would feel uneasy and nostalgic at heart. Others denied this and maintained that there was no feeling more noble or exquisite than that which followed each encounter with Bird; for then one's heart felt as it did after Holy Communion, or as after hearing a lovely song; one thought of all that was beautiful and ideal, and deep inside resolved to become a different and a better human being.

A man by the name of Schalaster, a cousin of the well-known Sehuster who for many years was the mayor of Montagsdorf, was all his life deeply and especially preoccupied with Bird. Every year, so he tells us, he would encounter Bird on one or two or several occasions. For days after each encounter he would find himself in strange spirits; he was not exactly cheerful, but rather oddly moved and full of expectation and surmise. On such days his heart beat in a different way from the usual, it almost hurt a little; in any case, he could feel it in his breast, whereas otherwise he was scarcely aware that he had a heart. When he came to speak of it, Schalaster opined that it was no mere trifle to have this bird in the neighborhood; one ought to be proud of this *rara avis*, and one ought to think: a person to whom this enigmatic bird had revealed himself more often than to others had no doubt something special and exalted in him.

(Better-educated readers will be interested in the following particulars about Schalaster. He was the star witness and the often-quoted authority in that eschatological treatise on the Bird phenomenon, which meanwhile has once again sunk into oblivion; moreover, after Bird's disappearance, Schalaster was the spokesman for that small faction in Montagsdorf which believed unconditionally that Bird was still alive and would reappear at some future time.)

"When I saw him for the first time," Schalaster relates,* "I was a little boy who had not yet entered school. In the orchard behind our house the grass had just been cut, and I was standing near a cherry tree, one of whose lower branches hung down almost to my height, looking at the hard, green cherries, when Bird came flying down from the tree. I realized at once that he was different from all the other birds I had seen, and he landed amid the grass stubble and hopped all around. With curiosity and admiration I ran after him through the garden; several times he looked at me out of his lustrous eyes and hopped farther away, it was as when someone dances and sings for himself alone, and it was quite clear to me that in doing so he meant to entice me and cheer me. There was a white patch on his neck. He went dancing over the lawn as far as the back fence where the nettles grow, soared over them and landed on one of the fence posts, where he twittered and gave me another friendly look, then he disappeared so suddenly and unexpectedly that I was quite

---

* See *Avis montagnolens*, res gestae ex recens. Ninonis, p. 285 ff.

alarmed. Even on subsequent encounters I often remarked this: no other animal can appear and disappear at such lightning speed as Bird—and always when one is least prepared for it. I ran indoors to my mother and told her what had happened; directly she told me that it was the bird with no name, and it was good that I had seen him; it brought good luck."

Departing somewhat from many other accounts, Schalaster describes Bird as small, scarcely larger than a wren, the smallest part of him being his head, a wonderfully clever and nimble little head. His appearance was unremarkable, but one recognized him right away by his gray-blond crest and by the way he looked at one, which other birds never do. The crest was, even if quite a bit smaller, like that of a jay, and it often bobbed up and down in a lively fashion; Bird was in general very animated, in flight as well as on foot. His movements were supple and very expressive; with his eyes, with the nodding of his head, with the bobbing of his crest, he always seemed to have something to communicate, something to remind you of, like a messenger always on an errand; and whenever you saw him, you had to stop for a while and think about him, what he might have wanted and what he signified. He did not like to have anyone spy on him or lie in wait for him, and no one ever knew where he had come from. Quite suddenly he would just be there, sitting nearby and acting as if he had always sat there, and then he would have this friendly look. And yet we know that birds, as a rule, have hard, shy, glassy eyes and do not look at people, but Bird looked at people quite cheerfully, and to a certain degree benevolently.

Even in olden times there were many and varying reports and legends about Bird. Today one hears less and less about him, people have changed and life has become harder; almost all young people go to work in the city, families no longer sit together on the outside stairs on summer evenings or around the hearth on winter evenings; no one has time for anything any more, a young person today scarcely knows a few wildflowers or a butterfly by name. Nonetheless, even today one occasionally hears an old woman or a grandfather telling stories about Bird to children. One of these legends about Bird, perhaps the oldest one, goes as follows.

Bird from Montagsdorf is as old as the world, he was there when Cain slew his brother Abel, and he drank a drop of Abel's blood; then he flew away with the tidings of Abel's death and he tells of it to people even today, so that they do not forget this story, and so they are constantly reminded of the sanctity of human life and the importance of living together as brothers.

This Abel legend had already been written down in olden times and there are songs about it. But the scholars say that although the legend of the Abel bird is indeed very old and has been told in many countries and many languages, its application to the Bird of Montagsdorf is fallacious. They would have people bear in mind that it would be completely absurd for this Abel bird, many thousands of years old, to settle down in this one region without ever having shown himself elsewhere.

Now, for our part, we certainly could bear in mind that in fairy tales things don't always necessarily happen as rationally as they do in the academies, and we could ask if it is not the scholars themselves who are responsible for so much uncertainty and so many contradictions in the matter of Bird; because before their time, to the best of our knowledge, there had never been disputes about Bird and his legends. If someone told a tale about Bird different from that of his neighbor, his version was calmly accepted; in fact, that people could think and tell so many diverse things about Bird only served to honor him. One could go even further and rebuke the scholars: not only should they have the extirpation of Bird on their conscience, but also in their present investigations they are guilty of endeavoring to efface all memory of him and his legends until nothing further remains, for it certainly seems that explication into nothingness is the special province of scholarship. But who among us would have the sad courage so grossly to attack the scholars, to whom knowledge owes, if not everything, so very much?

No, let us turn back to those legends told of Bird in former times, fragments of which are still being told today by the country folk. In most of them Bird is taken for an enchanted, transformed, or cursed being. The legend that Bird was an enchanted Hohenstaufen, the last great emperor or magus of the line that ruled in Sicily, who knew the secrets of Arabian wisdom, may well be due to the influence of those who made the Journey to the East, in whose history the region between Montagsdorf and Morbio plays a decisive role, and whose tracks one comes upon throughout the region. Generally it is said that Bird was once a prince, or even (as, for example, Sehuster believes he heard) a sorcerer, who lived in a red house on the Hill of Snakes and was held in high esteem by all who lived in the region. But then the new law of Flachsenfingen went into effect, which resulted in many going hungry, because sorcery, spell-casting, self-transformation, and other such arts were forbidden and marked with infamy. In those days the sorcerer had planted blackberries and acacias all around his red house, which soon disappeared in a thicket of thorns; he left his house and land and, accompanied by long trains of snakes, disappeared into the woods. As Bird, he returns from time to time to ensnare human souls and again to practice sorcery. Naturally, magic is the only explanation for the peculiar influence he exerted over so many; the storyteller is silent as to whether the sorcerer practiced magic of the white or the black variety.

Those remarkable fragmentary folktales which point toward a kind of matriarchal culture, and in which the "Foreign Woman," also called Ninon, plays a role, also indubitably exhibit the influence of those who made the Journey to the East. Many of these tales relate that she succeeded in catching Bird and holding him captive for years, until the village finally became indignant and set its bird free. There is also the rumor that the foreign woman Ninon had known Bird long before he had assumed the shape of a bird, while he was still a magus, and further that she lived with him in the red house, where they bred and raised long black snakes and green lizards with blue peacock's heads. Even today the Blackberry Hill above Montagsdorf is full of snakes, and even today one can distinctly see how every snake and every lizard, when it comes to the spot where the threshold of the sorcerer's workshop had been, pauses a moment, raises up its head, and then bows. Now long deceased, a very old woman from the village, Nina by name, is said to have told and sworn to the following tale. Very often, while out looking for herbs on the Hill of Thorns, she would see the vipers bow down at that place where even now the stump of a small rosebush, many hundreds of years old, marks the entrance to the former House of Magic. Yet other voices assert most definitely that Ninon had nothing whatsoever to do with the magus; she came to the region only much later, in the distant wake of those who made the Journey to the East, long after Bird had become a bird.

AN ENTIRE GENERATION has not yet gone by since the last time Bird was seen. But old people pass away so unexpectedly, even the "Baron" is gone now, and it has been a long time since the cheerful Mario walked without stooping, as we knew him to, and one day there will suddenly be no one left who experienced the days of Bird at first hand; that is why we want to write down the details of Bird's story, however confused they may seem, to record what happened to him and how he met his end.

Even if Montagsdorf lies rather far off the beaten path and relatively few people know the quiet little wooded ravines that surround it, where the kite rules the woods and the cuckoo's cry is heard everywhere, nonetheless it was there that the strange bird was often seen, and it was there that the legends about him sprang up. There it is said the painter Klingsor lived for many years in his noble old ruin; the gorge of Morbio became known through Leo's Journey to the East (moreover, in an even more absurd variant of the tale, it is said that Ninon obtained from Leo the recipe for bishop's bread, on which she fed Bird, and in doing so tamed him). In short, our region—which for centuries was utterly unknown and utterly irreproachable—was now under discussion throughout the world; far away in cities and at universities, people wrote dissertations on Leo's path to Morbio, and these people took an intense interest in the various stories of the Bird of Montagsdorf. And so all sorts of rash statements were made and written, statements which the more serious scholars of folklore are now at pains to suppress. Among others there arose more than once the absurd contention that Bird was identical with the famed Bird of Pictor, who had dealings with the painter Klingsor, and who possessed the gift of transformation as well as a great deal of secret knowledge. But that bird, famous through Pictor, that "Bird red and green; lovely, daring," is so precisely described in the literature* that one can scarcely comprehend the possibility of such a mistake.

And finally the learned world's interest in us natives of Montagsdorf and our Bird reached a climax, just as the story of Bird reached its own climax in the following way. One day, into the hands of our former mayor, the afore-mentioned Sehuster, there came a letter from the office immediately superior to his own. Addressing himself to the Current Occupant of the Office of Mayor of the Said Locality, His Grace the Ambassador of the Ostrogoth Empire, writing on behalf of Privy Councillor Lützkenstett the Erudite, sends the following communiqué to the mayor with the urgent request that he make known to his community the following proclamation: A certain bird with no name, commonly referred to as "the Bird of Montags-dorf," under the auspices of the Ministry of Culture, is being researched and sought after by Privy Councillor Lützkenstett. Whosoever has anything whatsoever to com-municate with respect to the bird, its habits, its diet, the maxims and proverbs, the legends and tales, etc., pertain-ing to it, should direct same through the Mayor's Office to the Imperial Ostrogothian Embassy in Bern. Further: whosoever shall deliver the bird in question, alive and in

---

* *Pictoris cuiusdam de mutationibus*, Bibl. av. Montagn. codex LXI.

good health, to the aforementioned Office of the Mayor, shall receive from the Embassy a consideration in the sum of one thousand gold ducats; while, for the delivery of the dead bird or its skin, only one hundred ducats will be offered in payment.

For a long time the mayor sat studying this official document. It seemed to him that the authorities were up to their old tricks again, and their request was uncalled for and ridiculous. Had this same request been addressed specifically to him, Sehuster, on behalf of the learned Goth, or even on behalf of the Ostrogothian Embassy, he would have dismissed it out of hand, without extending the courtesy of a reply, or he would have intimated in a few words that such foolishness would not be tolerated by Mayor Sehuster, and the gentlemen could all go jump in the lake. But, alas, this request came from his own superior; it was an order and he had to obey it. Even far-sighted old Balmelli, the town clerk, after reading the letter to himself at full arm's length, and suppressing the scornful smile which such affairs seemed to merit, attested: "We must obey, Herr Sehuster; there's nothing we can do. I will post it as an official notice."

After a few days' time, the whole community had read the poster on the notice board of the Town Hall: Bird was free as a bird, he was wanted abroad, and a price had been put on his head; the Swiss Confederation and the Canton had declined to offer asylum to the legendary Bird; as usual, they didn't give a damn about the common man and that which he loved and cherished. This, at least,

was the opinion of Balmelli and numerous others. Whoever wanted to catch the poor bird or shoot him to death
did so at the bidding of a large sum of money, and whoever succeeded in doing it would be a wealthy man.
Everyone talked about it, everyone stood near the Town
Hall, crowding around the notice board, expressing himself
in a lively manner. The young people were most pleased
of all; they decided immediately to set traps and to prepare twigs with birdlime. Old Nina shook her gray,
sparrow-hawk head and said: "It's a sin, and the Bundesrat
ought to be ashamed. These people would turn in the
Saviour Himself for a price. But they will not get him,
God be praised, they will not get him!"

As he read the poster, Schalaster, the mayor's cousin,
remained completely silent. Without uttering a word, he
read it over very carefully a second time, neglected to go
to church, where he had meant to go on that Sunday
morning, slowly walked toward the mayor's house, went
into its garden, changed his mind quite suddenly, turned
around, and ran home.

All his life, Schalaster had had a special relationship
with Bird. He had seen him more frequently and observed
him more closely than others had; he belonged, if one may
say so, to those who believed in Bird, who took him more
seriously and who ascribed to him a higher significance.
Thus, the proclamation pulled him violently in several
directions at once. At first, he felt just as old Nina and
the majority of the elder citizens who followed the old
ways did: he was shocked and indignant that, at the

request of outsiders, his Bird, the treasure and trademark of the village and the region, was to be turned in as a prisoner, or else killed! How could it happen that this rare and mysterious guest from the forests, this fabulous being known from time immemorial, through whom Montagsdorf had become both famous and ridiculed, and about whom so many different stories and tales had come down—how was it that now, for the sake of money and knowledge, this bird should be sacrificed to the cruel inquisitiveness of a scholar? It seemed scandalous and absolutely beyond belief. One was being asked to commit a sacrilege. And yet, on the other hand, if one weighed the matter carefully, putting each thing now into one, now into the other, pan of the scale—wasn't an extraordinary and radiant fate promised to the man who committed that sacrilege? And wasn't the capture of the exalted Bird presumably a task that required a special man, one chosen and predestined, one who had lived in a most secret and intimate relation to Bird since childhood, one whose fate was entwined with Bird's? And who could this chosen and unique man be, who else but he, Schalaster? And if it was a sacrilege and a crime to take Bird by force, a sacrilege comparable to Judas Iscariot's betrayal of the Saviour—hadn't even that betrayal, hadn't the Saviour's death and sacrifice been necessary and holy, predestined and prophesied from the most ancient times? Would it have, Schalaster asked himself and all the world, would it have availed in the least, could it have altered or hindered in the slightest God's decree and His work of salvation if that same Iscariot, on moral or rational grounds, had shunned his role and failed to go through with the betrayal?

Such were the paths Schalaster's thoughts took, and they upset him enormously. In that very same orchard behind his house, where once as a small boy he had seen Bird for the first time and had felt the tremor of joy of that adventure, he now paced back and forth in agitation, to the goat stall, to the kitchen window, to the rabbit coop and beyond, his Sunday coat grazing the hayrakes, pitchforks, and scythes hanging on the back wall of the barn—upset and confused, almost intoxicated with thoughts, wishes, and resolutions, heavyhearted, thinking of Judas, a thousand heavy dream-ducats in the bag.

Meanwhile, the excitement continued to spread through the village. Since the notice had been posted, practically the whole community had gathered in front of the Town Hall; from time to time, someone would walk up to the notice board and take another hard look at the poster. All came equipped with their own opinions and, using a few well-chosen words from personal experience, common sense, and the Holy Scriptures, they forcefully aired them. The proclamation had split the village into two opposing camps; there were only a few people who did not, immediately upon reading it, make up their minds one way or the other. No doubt there were those who, like Schalaster, considered the actual hunting of Bird a frightful thing, but who, nonetheless, would have liked to have the ducats, and not everybody was capable of carefully sorting out this complicated contradiction. The young men took it least

seriously. Considerations, moral or conservational, could
not in the least curb their spirit of adventure. In their
opinion, if traps were set, someone might be lucky enough
to catch Bird, even if there was little chance of it, since
no one knew what bait to use to attract Bird. And if someone managed to spot Bird, he would be well advised to
shoot on sight, because, after all, one hundred ducats in
one's wallet would be better than one thousand in one's
imagination. Loudly they agreed among themselves, and
looked forward to what they were going to do, but they
quarreled over the particulars of the bird hunt. One of them
cried out for someone to give him a good rifle, he would put
down one half ducat on account, he'd be ready to start
out at once and willing to sacrifice his whole Sunday to
the task. The opposition, however, whose ranks included
almost all of the old people, found the whole thing shock-
ing. They cried aloud or muttered words of wisdom and
maledictions on the people of today, to whom nothing was
sacred any more, who had lost all fidelity and belief.
Laughing, the young people retorted that this was not a
matter of fidelity or belief; rather, it was a matter of
marksmanship—of course, all virtue and wisdom would
continue to reside in those whose half-blind eyes no longer
could take aim at a bird, and whose gouty fingers no
longer could hold a rifle. And so it went back and forth,
with brio, and people exercised their wit on this new problem, so much so that they almost completely forgot to eat.
Passionately and eloquently, they told stories of good and
bad times in their families, stories more or less relating to

Bird; urgently they reminded everyone of holy grandfather Nathanael, of old Sehuster, of the fabulous pilgrimage of those who made the Journey to the East; they quoted verses from the psalm book and relevant passages from operas, found one another intolerable and yet could not leave one another's company, called upon the mottos and dicta of their forebears, delivered monologues on times gone by, on the dead bishop, on illnesses survived. A seriously ill old farmer, for example, who lay on his sickbed, looked out of his window and caught sight of Bird, only for a moment, but from that instant he began to recover. They spoke, partly to themselves—addressing an inner vision—and partly to their fellow villagers, imploring or accusing, concurring or deriding; in discord as in accord, they had a pleasant feeling of the strength, the endurance, the endlessness of their solidarity. The old and wise came forward, the young and clever came forward, teased one another, ardently and rationally defended the good old ways of their fathers, ardently and rationally questioned the good old ways of their fathers, boasted of their ancestors, smirked about their ancestors, celebrated their age and experience, celebrated their youth and their arrogance, let it almost come to blows, bellowed, laughed, assayed their common goals and disagreements, every one of them seemingly up to his neck in the conviction that he was right and that he had said something clever to the others.

In the midst of these verbal exercises and all this taking of sides, during which the ninety-year-old Nina adjured her blond grandson to heed her forebodings and not ally himself with these cruel and godless people in their dangerous hunt for Bird, and during which the young people disrespectfully acted out a pantomime of the hunt before her hoary countenance—placing imaginary rifles to her cheeks, squinting their eyes and taking aim, screaming pop! bang!—something quite unexpected happened, and young and old alike fell dumb in mid-sentence and stopped, as if turned to stone. Old Balmelli cried out, and all eyes turned to follow his outstretched arm and pointing finger, and—suddenly amid deep silence—they saw Bird, the much-discussed Bird himself, soar down from the roof of the Town Hall and land on the edge of the notice board, rub his wing against his round little head, whet his beak and chirp out a brief melody; batting his agile little tail up and down and trilling, he ruffled up his crest. And he—known only by hearsay to many of the villagers—groomed himself a little while right before everyone's eyes, showed himself, and bent down his head, as if he, too, were curious about the proclamation of the authorities, wanting to know how many ducats were being offered for him. He may only have paused there for a few moments, but to everyone present the visit seemed solemn and like a challenge; now no one cried out "pop, bang"; instead, they all stood and stared, as if spellbound, at the daring visitor who had come flying to them and who had chosen to appear at this place and this moment with the sole intention of making fun of them. Astonished and embarrassed, they stared at him who had taken them so by surprise; with delight and satisfaction they looked at the fine little fellow, about whom there had recently been so much talk and because of whom their region was famous, he who had been witness to Abel's death, or who had been a Hohenstaufen or a Prince or a Magus, and had lived in a red house on the Hill of Snakes, where even now vipers lived, at him who had aroused the curiosity and greed of foreign scholars and governments, at him for whose capture a reward of one thousand gold pieces was offered. They all loved and admired him, even those who just a few moments later would curse and stamp their feet in annoyance, because their hunting rifles were not at hand; they loved him and were proud of him, he belonged to them, he was their honor and their glory; batting his tail and ruffling his crest, he sat very close by, above their heads, on the edge of the notice board, like their prince or their coat of arms. And only now, when he suddenly disappeared and the spot everyone had been staring at was empty, did they slowly awaken from the spell cast over them. They laughed at one another, cried out "bravo," sang Bird's praises, called out for their rifles, asked in which direction he had flown, remembered that this was the same bird that had healed the old farmer, the one the grandfather of the ninety-year-old Nina had known, felt something strange, something like happiness and the desire to laugh, but at the same time something mysterious, magical, awe-inspiring; and suddenly they scattered in all directions, went home to their soup, at last to make an end of this exciting assembly in which the intense emotions of the whole village had been raised to the boiling point, emotions over which Bird obviously reigned king. In front of the Town Hall it grew still, and a while later, when the midday bells began to toll, the square lay utterly empty and lifeless. On the whiteness of the sun-lit poster, a shadow then began to fall, the shadow of the molding of the notice board, on which not a moment ago Bird had been sitting.

In the meantime Schalaster, lost in thought, was pacing up and down behind his house, past the rakes and the scythes, past the stalls for the rabbits and the goats; his steps gradually became less agitated and more uniform, his theological and moral ponderings coming closer and closer to equilibrium and stasis. The midday bells aroused him; startled and sobered, he returned to the present, recognized the call of the bells, knew that in a moment his wife would call him to the table, was a little ashamed at his self-absorption, and stepped more firmly in his boots. And now, just as his wife's voice was raised, confirming the call of the village bells, all at once something seemed to swim before his eyes. A whirring sound whizzed close by and went past him, something like a brief gust of air, and in the cherry tree sat Bird; light as a blossom on a branch he sat and playfully batted his feathered crest, turned his little head, peeped gently, looked into the man's eyes—Schalaster had known Bird's look since childhood—and already he hopped away again and vanished in the branches and the breezes, even before the staring Schalaster had time to properly perceive the faster beating of his own heart.

After that Sunday noon when Bird appeared in Schalaster's cherry tree, only once more was he ever seen by human eyes; and, in fact, on that occasion again by that very same Schalaster, cousin of the former mayor. He had firmly made up his mind to seize Bird and get the ducats; and since he, the old bird specialist, knew for certain that Bird would never be captured, he had readied an old rifle and procured a store of shot of the finest caliber, the kind known as bird shot. If things went according to his plans and he were to shoot at Bird with this fine shot, it was plausible that Bird would not fall down dead, and blasted to pieces, but rather that one of the tiny little grains of shot would wound him only slightly and that he would be stunned with terror. In that way it would be possible to take Bird alive. The prudent man got everything ready in advance, including a little songbird cage in which to lock up the prisoner, and from that moment on he tried his utmost never to be far from his perpetually loaded rifle. Wherever he could, he took it with him, and where he could not take it—to church, for example—he was loath to go.

In spite of all these preparations, when the moment came and he met up with Bird again—it was in the autumn of that same year—he did not quite have his rifle at hand. It happened very near to Schalaster's house. As was his wont, Bird had appeared without a sound, and after landing, he greeted Schalaster with his familiar chirping; Bird sat cheerfully on the gnarled stump of a bough of an old willow tree, a tree from which Schalaster always cut branches to use to espalier the wall fruit. There

Bird

Bird sat, not ten paces away, chirping and chattering, and
his foe once again felt that strange sensation of joy in his
heart (blessed and wretched at once, as if he were being
asked to live a life he was not yet capable of living), even
while the sweat ran down his neck, for he was worried
and anxious about how he could get to his gun in time.
He rushed into the house, came back with his rifle, saw
that Bird was still sitting in the willow, and now he stalked
him; slowly and stepping lightly, he came closer and
closer. Bird was unsuspecting, worried neither by the rifle
nor by the strange deportment of the man—an agitated
man with a fixed stare, ducking movements, and a bad
conscience—who evidently was taking great pains to pre-
tend disinterest. Bird let him come closer, looked at him
confidingly, tried to cheer him up, gave him a roguish
look, while the farmer raised his rifle, squinted one eye,
and took a long time aiming. At last the shot cracked, and
scarcely had the cloud of smoke dispersed than Schalaster
was on his knees searching under the willow. From the
willow to the garden fence and back, to the beehives and
back, to the bed of beans and back, he scoured the grass,
every handsbreadth of it, twice, three times, for an hour,
for two hours, and again and again on the next day. He
could not find Bird, he could not find a single one of his
feathers. Bird had taken to his heels, things had gone off
too clumsily, the report of the gun had been too loud, Bird
loved freedom, he loved the peace and quiet of the woods,
he was no longer happy here. He was gone, and on this
occasion too, Schalaster had not been able to see in which

(165

direction he had flown. Perhaps he had returned to his house on the Hill of Snakes, where the blue-green lizards would bow down to him at the threshold. Perhaps he had flown even farther back in space and time, to the Hohenstaufen, to Cain and Abel, into Paradise.

From that day on, Bird was never seen again. There was still a lot of talk about him; even today, after so many years, it has not yet been silenced; and in an Ostrogothian university town a book about him was published. If in the old days all sorts of legends about him were told, since the time of his disappearance Bird himself has become a legend, and soon there will be no one left who can attest that Bird ever actually existed, that he was once the benevolent spirit of the region, that a high price was put on his head, that he had been shot at. At some time in the future, when still another scholar researches this legend, all this will perhaps be labeled an invention of the popular imagination, accounted for, feature by feature, by the laws of mythmaking. For it cannot be denied that all over the world and in all ages there are beings who are perceived to be extraordinary, charming, and appealing, and whom many honor as benevolent spirits, because they make one think of a more beautiful, a freer, a more winged life than the one we lead. And the same thing always happens: the grandsons deride the good genies of their grandfathers, one day the extraordinary beings are hunted and shot dead, prices are put on their heads or their hides, and not long afterwards their existence turns into a legend, which with the wings of a bird flies ever further away.

166)

Bird

No one can predict what forms all this information about Bird will assume in the future. That Schalaster perished in a terrible manner, most probably a suicide, should be reported for the sake of completeness, but we will not permit ourselves to append any further commentary on this incident.

Nocturnal Games

DECADES HAVE PASSED since I made a consistent practice of recalling my nightly dreams, mentally reproducing them, at times even writing them down; and using the method I learned back then, I would examine them for their meaning, or at least listen to them and track them down until something like a reminder, a sharpening of my instincts, a warning, or encouragement would result, depending on the circumstances, but in all cases a greater intimacy with the realms of dream, a better exchange between the conscious and the unconscious than one, as a rule, possesses. My acquaintance with a few books on the subject and my firsthand experience of undergoing psychoanalysis were more than a mere sensation, they were encounters with forces that were very real.

But just as happens with even the most intensive pursuit of knowledge, the most ingenious and most thrilling course of instruction through men or books, so, too, it happened, as the years passed, with this encounter with the world of dream and the unconscious: life went on, always making new demands and posing new questions; the highly unnerving and sensational nature of that initial encounter lost its novelty and its demand for commitment, the totality of the analytical experience could not go on being cultivated as an end in itself, it was put in its place, to some extent it was forgotten or else superseded by life's new demands, but without ever entirely losing its quiet efficacy and power; just as perhaps in the life of a young man, the first books he reads by Hölderlin, Goethe, Nietzsche, his first experiences with the opposite sex, his first awakening to social or political consciousness must be coordinated with his past body of experience.

SINCE THAT TIME I have grown old, but the ability to address myself through dreams and at times gently to be instructed or guided by them has never left me completely; but neither has the dream life ever again regained the pressing urgency and importance it once had for me. Since then, there have been times when I have remembered my dreams, alternating with others in which I have lost all trace of them by morning. Nonetheless, time and again, dreams continue to surprise me—and, to be sure, the dreams of others no less than my own—because of their indefatigability and the inexhaustibility of their creative and playful imagination, because of their simultaneously childlike and ingenious way of combining disparate elements, and because of their often enchanting humor.

As an artist I have also been influenced by a certain intimacy with the dream world and much brooding over the artistic aspects of the art of dreaming (yet another one of the arts which psychoanalysis has not yet properly understood, or dealt with more than in passing). In art I have always enjoyed playfulness; even as a boy and as a young man, I frequently and with great pleasure practiced a kind of surrealistic method of composition, mostly for myself alone; I still do so today—for example, in the early morning hours when I cannot sleep—but of course I don't write down these soap-bubble creations. By playing these games, and by reflecting on the dream's naïve sleights of hand and on surrealistic art's unnaïve ones—the partaking in which and the practice of which gives so much pleasure and requires so little effort—it has also become clear to me why, as a poet, I may have to forgo the practice of this kind of art. I allow myself to do it with a clear conscience only in the private sphere—during the course of my life I have made thousands of surrealistic verses and pronouncements, and still go on doing so, but the kind of artistic ethics and responsibility I have arrived at over the years would no longer allow me to employ this private and irresponsible technique in my serious oeuvre today.

Now, these *raisonnements* cannot be enlarged upon here. If once again I am concerning myself with the world of dreams, it is not with intentions, designs, and intellectual goals, but simply because within the last few days I have been stimulated by encounters with several peculiar dreams.

I had the first dream on the night of a day on which I had pains and great fatigue. I was severely depressed, my life worthless; and hindered in my repose by shooting pains in my limbs, I lay down and slept. And in this bad, sullen sleep I dreamed precisely what I in actuality was doing: I dreamed that I was lying in bed, sleeping heavily and badly, but in an unknown place, in a strange room and bed. I went on dreaming that in the strange room I awakened from my sleep; slowly, reluctantly, and fatigued I awakened, and through the veils of tiredness and a feeling of dizziness it took me a long time to become aware of my situation. Slowly my consciousness struggled and spiraled upward, slowly and grudgingly I conceded that I was now awake, unfortunately after a counterfeit, difficult, profitless sleep which had worn me out more than it refreshed me.

And so now (in the dream) I was awake, slowly opened my eyes, slowly raised myself up a little on my arms, which had gone to sleep and lost all sensation; through the strange window I saw gray daylight fall, and suddenly I was jolted, something disquieting went through me, something like anxiety or a bad conscience, and I hastily made a grab for my pocket watch to see what time it was. Sure enough, confound it, it was past ten, almost ten-thirty, and indeed for months now I had been a student or a guest at a Gymnasium, where I was diligently and heroically trying to make good on some old omission, and I wanted to attend the last classes. My God, it was ten-thirty, and I should have been in school at eight o'clock; and even if I could once again present my excuses to the headmaster as I had done just the other day, attributing my failure to the increasing impediments of old age—yes, his understanding was something I could count on—still, I had just missed the morning lecture and was not at all certain that I'd be well enough to attend school in the afternoon;

and all the while the class went on, and the possibility of my going to it grew more and more doubtful. And now there suddenly appeared to be some kind of startling explanation for the fact that in these last couple of months since I had reenrolled in the Gymnasium, much to my dismay, I still had not had a single Greek lesson, and in my heavy briefcase, which was often so laborious to carry, I had never been able to find a Greek grammar. Oh, perhaps there was nothing in my noble resolution to make amends for my neglected duties to the world and to school, and to still make something of myself; and perhaps even the headmaster, who had always shown me so much understanding, and who also knew me, to some extent, from reading a few of my books, had for a long time or even from the outset been convinced of the absurdity of my undertaking. In the end, would it not perhaps be better to lay the watch aside, close my eyes again, and spend the entire morning in bed, perhaps the afternoon as well, and thereby admit that I had set out to do something impossible? In any case, there was no longer any point in pulling myself together for the morning, it was already wasted. And scarcely had I thought these thoughts than I awakened in reality, saw a thin ray of light coming from the window, and found myself in my own room and my own bed, knew that breakfast and a lot of mail were waiting for me downstairs, and reluctantly I got up from this sleep and this dream, in no way fortified, rather astonished and somewhat inclined to laugh at myself, because this ingenious dream had put me in front of a mirror and in so doing had made such sparing use of surrealistic artifice.

A few days later, I had scarcely let this dream—so realistic, so unpoetic, so unlike a fable—subside and had almost forgotten it, when another dream addressed itself to me, but this one was poetic and amusing, and not one of my own. Rather, it came from a woman I do not know, one of my readers who lived in some small town in northern Germany. She had had the dream some twelve years before, but had never forgotten it, and only now had it occurred to her to communicate it to me. I now quote the letter itself verbatim:

"No bigger than Tom Thumb, I was on a gardener's hat you were wearing. You were planting shrubs, and I knew that you were mixing earth with water and kneading the two together. I could not see this, the broad brim of the hat prevented my seeing. Before my eyes lay a wonderful terraced landscape. When you stooped down, I ran, somewhat anxiously, as if on an unsteady chain bridge, toward the back of your hat, so as not to slip off. And from time to time I had to take shelter under the bow on one side of the hatband, when one of your hands reached up menacingly to secure the hat on your head. I thought it was great fun that you hadn't the slightest inkling of my presence. My joy increased when the glorious song of a bird began to sound. In the dark foliage of a tree I saw the Firebird glowing and said softly to myself: 'If only H. Hesse knew that it is the Firebird singing! He's thinking,

it is Papageno.' In some way I took comfort from it all:
the landscape, my dwarf existence on the huge hat, the
song of the bird, your working in the garden, and even
your being mistaken about the Firebird."

Now, this really was quite a lovely dream, and also an
amusing one. And because it was not one of my own I felt
no impulse to understand and interpret it. I took nothing
but pleasure in it, but later on I still thought, God alone
knows whether or not it was Papageno!

As if this stranger's dream—which, from my standpoint,
was so much prettier and more harmless than my own—
had aroused my own capacity to dream or made it ambitious, immediately afterward I myself dreamed up a dream;
to be sure, this one was not really beautiful or clever, but it
was truly fantastic.

I was in the midst of a number of people on one of the
upper floors of a large house, and I knew it was a theater
in which *Steppenwolf* was to be performed; someone had
adapted it as a play or an opera. Obviously, it was the
premiere performance, to which I had been invited; and
the proceedings on stage were familiar to me, but I could
neither see nor hear them at all; I sat in a kind of niche,
as if I were in the choir loft of a church, hidden behind the
organ. There were quite a few of these niches up there;
like so many trellises, they seemed to surround the actual
auditorium, and now and then I would get up and go
looking for a seat from which one could see the stage; but
no such place could be found, we were sitting around
rather like people who arrive too late and only know that

behind the closed doors the performance goes on. But I knew the upcoming scenes were those on which the adaptors and producers had spared no expense on music, sets, or lighting, creating something which with loathing I term "grand theatrics," something I would have liked to prevent. I began to feel uneasy. Then Dr. Korrodi came up to me smiling and said: "You can rest easy, no need to worry about an empty house." I said: "That may be so, but all this theatrical to-do simply ruins the third act for me."

There was no further discussion. Gradually it dawned on me that this curious piece of architecture, which one could not see over and which separated the actual theater from me, was an organ, and again I got going, trying to find my way around it in the hope of discovering a way into the auditorium. I did not succeed, but on the other side of this organ construction, which reminded me a great deal of a library, I came upon a piece of equipment, a machine, an apparatus, that to some extent resembled a bicycle; at least it had two large wheels of equal size, and above them was something like a saddle. And all at once it was clear to me: if you sat up there in the saddle and got the wheels turning, then, through some kind of tube, you could see as well as hear what was going on onstage.

This was a solution, and it made me feel better. But the dream offered nothing further in the way of resolution or satisfaction; it was content to have invented this ingenious machine, and it was happy to leave me standing in front of it. For, to reach the rather high saddle, placed well up above the wheels, certainly did not seem an easy thing to do, except for young people who, moreover, were cyclists. And the saddle was never empty; whenever I got ready to start climbing into it, there was always somebody there ahead of me. And so I stood and stared at the saddle and the wondrous tube, through whose narrow shaft one could see as well as hear what was going on in the theater, where all the while the third act was being ruined by the experts. I was neither upset nor sad, really, but it seemed to me that some kind of hoax or deception had been perpetrated, and although the dramatization of *Steppenwolf* throughout was not to my liking, I would have given something to have succeeded in getting into the theater itself, or at least up into the saddle above the wonder-working tube. Nothing, however, came of it.

Report from Normalia

(A Fragment from the Year 1948)

M Y DEAR, most devoted, and highly esteemed Friend, because in your goodness you encourage me to do so, I will resume our correspondence—which has always seemed on my part more like a monologue than a dialogue, and which has been broken off during these years of terrible misfortune—and once again I will report to you about my life and the general state of affairs here in Normalia. Admittedly, you may well be better informed than I about our state and its establishments, hemmed in as I am by my own subjectivity; I feel very much at home here, even if something peculiar, contradictory, or alienating in our community and our way of life now and then makes me feel surprised or shocked, derided or deceived, or even led about by the nose. Well now, that's how it is here, and probably it is and was like this everywhere and at all other times on earth; and, as I've already said, I am comfortable here and have neither the intention nor the need to criticize or complain of conditions here. On the contrary, in our far-reaching Institution, the quality of life is good; and the riddles posed by our life in Normalia perhaps are not so very different from those in your own Nordblock,

or whatever name your country may go by nowadays. We
are, for example, preoccupied with and unsettled by the
question of who now holds the position of Director——but
for the moment, let me remain silent on this all-important
matter. There is another question about which we are but
meagerly informed: how, since the downfall of the last
Tyrannis, did we arrive at the present Dictatorship of the
Classes, as we ourselves officially designate it? But you are
probably far more interested in another question, or rather
a complex of questions, in that very question which
touches on the legends of the early history of our Institution—or more properly, our wide-ranging and densely
populated community. As you know, we of Normalia live
here as voluntary, autonomous, self-governing inmates of
a network of provinces which belongs to the West–Eastern
Federal Dictatorial Conglomerate of States. However, the
cradle of our country and community was a small land-
scaped park, scarcely encompassing one square mile of
ground in the north of Aquitaine; and at the time of the
last political and martial upheavals, this park with its
dozen or so buildings was nothing other than a medium-
sized, very well run Insane Asylum. The official historians
explain our asylum's transformation into an autonomous
state and country as follows: since the beginning of the
Glorious Epoch, there has been an enormous rise in anxiety
and other mass psychoses, in consequence of which the
famed Asylum was beset by a huge influx of patients; thus,
out of the settlement arose a village, a complex of villages,
finally a complex of districts and cities, and soon our

country as we now know it had come into being. Along with it there sprang up a system of institutions, corresponding to the needs of the richly varied categories of patients, institutions for the seriously and less-seriously disturbed, for addicts, for neurotics, for the merely nervous, etc., etc.; and while, then as now, the various asylums for the seriously ill were under the direction of doctors who followed the principles of the psychiatric practice of their day, all around these homes sprang up a little world of settlements and communal residences, in which there was neither doctor nor psychiatric practice, and which—owing to their rather pleasant living conditions—experienced a huge influx of people seeking peace and quiet, people from all parts of the Western world. And so it happened, so we believe and so the legend tells us, that not long after the stabilization of the W.–E. Conglomerate of States, our community came into existence, founded on the principle of a dictatorship of the classes, an Institute comprising thirty million reasonable and rational inmates, one into which every reasonable and rational man, provided he has passed certain tests and fulfilled certain requirements, has the right to enter. Thus it is in opposition to the original designation of our Asylum that our Institute-which-has-been-expanded-into-a-State unites the healthy and the normal; the remaining and far greater part of the Conglomerate, whose member states have been blown together by the east and the west winds, is populated and ruled by the more or less sick and disturbed. So says the legend, and basically we are satisfied with it and believe in it, just as every living creature must and does believe in its own existence. Only in more recent times, hand in hand with other irritating theories and notions, another troublesome notion has crept into our heads: An age-old characteristic symptom of the insane is the delight they take in appearing and posing as normal, healthy people; and so the notion has arisen among us that we are by no means reasonable and rational, rather that we are of unsound mind, our state is no state at all; in fact, we are quite simply inmates of an enormous asylum full of madmen. As I've already said, this is the single question which only a few of us from time to time seriously contemplate; but of course this pertains to the more refined and gifted among us, and the question of whether it is we or the others who are the madmen constitutes the principal subject matter of the philosophies and speculations of our men of genius. We others, we who are older and more detached, usually hold ourselves more to the general rules of the game and either believe purely and simply in the legend as handed down, hence in our sanity and the voluntary nature of our sojourn in Normalia, or else we are of the opinion that it would be pointless to distress ourselves with questions that cannot be answered, and it matters little to determine whether one is crazy or normal, whether one is the monkey in the cage or the gawking member of the Zoological Gardens who stares in through the bars from outside; rather, it is more proper and fitting to see Existence as well as Metaphysics as a game, one far from problem-free, but genuinely meaningful and charming, and to be glad of the many good and beautiful things we can experience while playing it. Nonetheless, as concerns the person and functions of our Herr Director, I must admit that even I have entertained all sorts of doubts and perhaps impudently have tried my own hand at penetrating the veil of mystery which surrounds him. But of that I shall not, for the time being, say another word; so much still remains to be clarified and settled before one can even venture to tackle this most delicate problem with the crude means of language and logic. Let us, venerable Patron, confine ourselves to the near and apparently clear, and let us, as far as possible, try to contain our speculations within proper bounds.

At present, after many changes of domicile, I live once again, as I did years ago, in the actual heart of Normalia, in one of the newer buildings on the grounds of the former Insane Asylum, not far from the hedge that separates the famous old park from the large kitchen garden. This place of residence, like all others in our State, has its advantages and disadvantages, its special local traditions, privileges, and obligations; for in a still relatively young federation of states, comprised of diverse districts, each with its individual early history, even the most powerful Constitution and ideology cannot succeed in annihilating the persistent, strong, provincial, individual ways of life. For example, we inmates of old- or Ur-Normalia don't have to trouble ourselves very much about civic duties; that is to say, we have the right but not the obligation to vote; and the most important civic function, the payment of taxes, is taken

care of for us by the Institution's managers; we don't need
to worry about it. As long as we still have a credit balance,
the sums are charged to our accounts; when this credit
balance is exhausted, the state sends us—so that once
again we can become sources of revenue—to another locality, placing us in any one of a number of different
trades—of course, in strict accordance with the principle
of voluntary self-determination. At present, to the best of
my knowledge, my credit balance will suffice for many
another quarterly bill and tax payment, unless once again
we find ourselves in one of those extremely serious crises
in which the entire population rises up in unanimous re-
volt and takes its collective fortune to the Offices of the
Tax Authorities, forcing the authorities to accept it under
threat of possible violence, to the great displeasure of the
civil servants—for, under our Constitution, whenever the
State becomes Sole Owner of all individual fortunes, all
civil servants are dismissed, there being nothing more for
them to collect. But these are arrangements with which
you, esteemed Friend, presumably are far better acquainted
than I, for even as an inhabitant of today's fully perfected
conglomerate state, I have become, to some extent, an
individualist and a dreamer, an ignorant and noncom-
mitted follower. After such a long interruption of our correspondence, allow me first of all to reestablish our former
intimacy and get on with my story, and perhaps I will be
able to tell you something interesting; I mean particulars
of my own and our communal life which may strike you
as new and amusing.

Report from Normalia

Among these many particulars is one I've already hinted at: the existence of the many regional peculiarities and special laws in our various districts, provinces, and cities; peculiarities conditioned by historical and in part ancient traditions, which, in spite of the voluntary dictatorial union, persist with great tenacity. So, for example, three or four years ago I was exhorted by the authorities to voluntarily and spontaneously effect a change of my place of residence, and to go to the city of Flachsenfingen, about which I had read many interesting things. I had leased and settled down in a garden pavilion, had gone for a few strolls; but no sooner had I sat down on an inviting park bench and started to write down a few lines of poetry than a policeman on a motorcycle came storming toward me at the speed of a gale wind; he asked me what I was doing.

"I'm writing a poem," I said, "if you've nothing against it."

"Oh," he said, a note of correction in his voice, "I would scarcely be worthy of my office if I had nothing against it. Writing poetry, you say? Now, let's see some proof of your qualifications, your permit. How about your guild card?"

Abashed, I confessed that I possessed no such thing, but I allowed myself to add that, to my knowledge, nowhere in the Constitution of Normalia was it written that one was obligated to join or show proof of membership in a guild.

"Are you trying to teach me what I already know?" he cried indignantly. "Forget about Normalia, we are in Flachsenfingen. Are you trying to tell me that you haven't got any papers? That you don't belong to a guild at all?"

That, in fact, was my case exactly, and now I learned that in this city nothing was as absolutely taboo and impossible as practicing any profession whatsoever without belonging to a guild. I had to hand over my paper and pencil and follow the severe man to the Town Hall, where I was brought before the mayor—he was actually quite a congenial man; I had to answer his numerous questions, and after I had grasped what all this was about, I asked whether I was to be assigned to the Poetic or Literary Guild. Now it was he who was somewhat embarrassed, because there was no such guild in his city. After I had been obliged to take an oath not to practice any profession whatsoever until I was assigned to a guild, the town council was convened; following a long-winded and lively debate, it was decided that I seemed best suited for the Tailors Guild, which thus ought to be asked to instate me. A few days went by before the chief officers of the Tailors Guild sought me out and told me that actually they neither could nor wanted to take up the statutes of their guild with me, but their eldest member had just died and thus there was an opening for me, provided that I would be approved by a unanimous vote of the full membership and was willing to guarantee my obedience to the laws of the guild. Of course I gave them my word on it all, as long as it was consistent with my honor as a human being and a poet. And after another meeting, at which I was brought up before the guild for questioning, I was invited on a trial basis to attend one of the solemn ceremonies of the guild; namely, the funeral of the eldest guild brother. So, somewhat faint of heart, I marched in the funeral procession behind the guild's banner, which was said to have been donated during the golden age of Flachsenfingen, under the auspices of Foreign Minister Richter. After the services had taken place and we had lain down our garlands, we went to the Linden to have a light meal with good white wine, of which we drank quite a bit. I took advantage of the gay, relaxed, lighthearted mood that had set in to take one of the worthy men aside and ask him if my prospects for membership appeared to be good.

"Ah," he said benevolently, "and indeed, why not? So far, you have pleased us quite well; and that we've never before had a poet as a member is basically no obstacle. Frankly speaking, for my own part, it has always been my opinion up until now that a poet is someone who has written his collected works and has been dead for quite some time. Now you, on your part, ought to do something that will ingratiate you and demonstrate your good intentions."

I explained that from the bottom of my heart I was prepared to do so, and asked him to advise me how I could best introduce myself to the gentlemen.

"Well," he said, "it doesn't have to cost you the whole world. For example, you could tap on your glass, stand up, and say to them that in sympathy with the guild and its senior member—who now rests in the bosom of God—it would give you pleasure to compose a poem about the deceased and to pay for today's consumption of wine."

"The idea of paying for the wine," I said gratefully, "appeals to me a great deal. But how shall I compose a poem about a dead old man whom I did not know, never saw, and about whom I know nothing, except that he was a tailor and had the honor of belonging to your guild?"

"You are a stranger here," my patron said. "Otherwise, you would know that our senior member was no more a tailor than the guild master or I or any of the other members. You yourself certainly are no tailor and yet you, too, want to become a member of our guild."

"But what then was the dead man's profession?"

"I don't know exactly, I believe that formerly he was the manager or the owner of a liquor concern; he was an educated man with impeccable manners. But you don't need to be so worried about your poem, you don't have to put a tailor in it, only perhaps the red silk banner with golden scissors; and you should make some lovely statement about death and human life and reunions and the like. That's what people like to hear on such occasions."

He began to grow impatient; we were standing in the doorway to the inn, and inside the cozy little parlor the glasses were ringing. I did not have the courage to detain him any longer and I let him get back to his friends; after a while I followed him meekly, but I found that, with the rolls and the good wine, gradually my courage and my good spirits were reviving. I stood up and extemporaneously composed a rhapsodic ode, and perhaps it is a pity that it was never written down. It had more power, verve, and a broader popular appeal than any of my other poems, and the men were exceedingly pleased with it. They became quite pensive; deeply moved, they nodded heartily in agreement; they cried out "bravo" and got up all together to clink glasses with me, to compliment me, and to bid me welcome as a member of their guild. I was moved to tears, and after all the handshaking I was about to announce that the wine was on me, when, in one of those moments of great clarity—which, after a lot of drinking, can blaze up like lightning—it came to me that the contents of my rather slender wallet might not—indeed, no longer could—suffice to pay for the wine. And so I remained silent; overwhelmed and happy, I mutely raised my glass to the many who were drinking my health. They were honored to take me into their time-honored guild: I was safe, never again would my work be under surveillance or forbidden; everything had been done in accordance with form and order.

And yet, never again did I hear from the Tailors Guild. This was the one and only time that I followed its lovely silk flag, the one time that I—a non-tailor among non-tailors—had partaken of rolls and wine with them, had regaled the guild brothers with verses and fraternized with them. On a few rare occasions it has happened that a face seemed familiar to me, and I have pondered over whether it might belong to one of my fellow guild members; but the owner of the face soon went past me and vanished. And so, of the whole experience, nothing has stuck with me but the memory of those two hours in the circle of the bereaved revelers.

Now, as concerns the poem I produced on that occasion in such an unusual fashion and which met with such thunderous applause, after more sober consideration I must say: it is better, it is a blessing that it was never written down and that no record of it exists. It was a product of circumstances which did not suit me and which all my life I have made many a sacrifice to avoid and prevent. The poem arose out of my forced accommodation to a situation which I found strange and unsuitable; and it arose out of a state of intoxication, which, to be sure, had less to do with the excellent white wine—of which I have nothing but the most pleasant memory—and far more to do with the unaccustomed atmosphere of fellowship, a feeling of belonging, of community, breast to breast and shoulder to shoulder—a good climate perhaps for politicians, pastors, and the lions of the lecture halls, but not for poets or people with similar callings, for whom not society but seclusion and solitude are salutary. That poem which seemed so beautiful and was such a great success I have indeed forgotten, which in itself proves that the verses were bad; but I have not forgotten—rather, it is with some amount of remorse and shame that it has stuck in my memory—the final sentiments of that rhymed sermon, the foolish and fainthearted, disagreeable and tasteless thoughts that certainly Death awaited us all, but it would be some consolation to know that once the grave had swallowed us up, our comrades, rallied around the dear old flag, would remember and memorialize us by making a libation. Such oil, such unctuous nonsense flowed from my lips, to the great delight of those honorable men who sat around the table, and whose hearts beat higher because of it; and just as my feeling of membership and security in this circle had been a fraud, leaving me feeling just as alone, wary, and suspicious of the magic of fellowship as I had always been, so, too, presumably, had the others' enthusiasm, camaraderie, and human kindness been a soap bubble and a pretty lie. And if later on I was really quite pleased that my membership in the guild of "tailors" entailed no further annoyances—no new gatherings, fraternizings, and ceremonies would take place, no entanglements and obligations would present themselves to me, still it was also the case that the others, my cherished brothers and fellow tailors, the deeply moved and gratefully enthusiastic auditors of my verses, the stouthearted shakers of my hands, later on really didn't give a damn about me. Once again society, the general public, the official world had approached me with menacing demands; after the appearance of the policeman on the clattering motorcycle, it seemed as if once again the world wanted either to forbid me to practice my profession or else to make me pay for the toleration of it with disproportionate, colossal, and intolerable sacrifices—and then all this culminated in a ceremony and a joke; the world wanted nothing more of me than two or three hours of drinking in a room full of harmless people, who on the next day no longer knew me and no longer required that I recognize them; all this was precisely the loveliest, the most delightful part of my guild story.

This, esteemed Friend, was what happened to me in Flachsenfingen. Altogether different things transpired shortly thereafter, when, once again exhorted to effect a voluntary and spontaneous change of residence, I resettled, this time in the Western Cultural District. This district enjoyed a reputation for intense cultural activity and an enterprising spirit, and this was a determining factor in my choice of it; moreover, there was the widespread if unsubstantiated rumor that the Director of Normalia, whose name is mentioned only with awe and respect, frequently sojourns here. Frankly speaking, considerations primarily opportunistic decided me in my attempt to resettle in the Western District. My personal finances needed to be put in order. In Flachsenfingen, not only could I not succeed in earning any income to speak of, but I had also run up debts; and after a comparatively short stay there, the invitation I received to change my place of residence voluntarily could probably be attributed more to these economic irregularities than to other causes. Now, according to all my sources, if they did not lie, the arts and sciences were appreciated and flourishing in the Western District; schools, universities, nurturing of the arts, museums, libraries, publishing houses, and newspaper chains were said to be on a high plane of development in this district, and there were also supposed to be competitions, state commissions, and academies here. If I succeeded in establishing myself and again bringing respect to my name, once so well known, it would be on the grounds of my accomplishments, or on the grounds of my formerly respected place in the world of letters, and if this was so, material success could not long elude me. Furthermore, whether I would remain in the Western District as a respected, safe and secure, successful man and live a happy and contented life, paying high taxes and enjoying high esteem, or whether on the other hand I would take all I had earned there and return to the cherished landscape of my Ur-Normalia and live or pension myself off there for life, did not for the time being concern me very much. The powerful attraction of the park, the ovum of our state, had never entirely released me from its spell; and with all due respect for the spiritual full bloom of the Cultural District, still the joy of swimming along in a stream of assiduous cultural activity did not appear to me unconditionally worth all the concomitant efforts; this "joy" had to mean more to younger, more ambitious people than to us old folk who love peace and quiet. But, on the other hand, the Western District had a strong attraction for me —owing to those aforementioned rumors concerning the special relationship between the Director of the Realm and this particular province. To learn more of him, the great unknown one, to establish a relationship with him or even with one of his high functionaries and co-workers, and to be able to penetrate even one of the many mysteries surrounding him, conceivably could have meant a great deal to me, as it could have to you, esteemed Patron. I only had to wait a few days in the Flachsenfingen Holding Station for Voluntary Emigrants, until a transport left for the Western Cultural District. The bus probably held be-

tween thirty and forty passengers, all of us intellectuals or
artists, except for two young people with cheerful and
pleasant faces and manners, who, as I learned from a
fellow passenger, a journalist, should be classed among
the barbarians. These two young people were more to my
liking than the majority of my colleagues, among whom
only two seemed really congenial, two men with long gray
hair and long gray beards, typifying a kind of artist—long
forgotten and only seldom encountered nowadays—who,
by hair, beard, and manner of dress, betoken a noble seclusion from the world and a harmless absentmindedness,
and for which I must ashamedly admit I have always felt a
certain sympathy. Of course, just now the young barbarians were eyeing these two noble, reclusive, beautiful graybeards with scorn and undisguised contempt on account
of their outmoded frisures and habiliments. The cheerful
youths simply did not know enough to recognize the artistic
tradition which the excellent graybeards, at least in their
outward appearance, called upon themselves to continue.
Moreover, the communicative journalist informed me that
one of these silver-haired men was a colleague of mine, a
poet. And while we stopped for gas and food and were
being fed in the tavern of an inn, I had the good fortune
to be able to cast a glance at what seemed to be a poetic
composition he had only recently begun. He was seated
right next to me, and before him on the table was a little
notebook. It was still new and empty; only the first page
was inscribed with a few lines penned in a coquettish cal-

ligraphy—lines which, my spy eyes whetted by curiosity, I managed to decipher. They read:

Papagallo
A short time ago, or so we hear tell, a parrot was born in the vicinity of Morbio; one who, while still in school, already so far surpassed his brothers and colleagues in age, wisdom, understanding, virtue, and goodwill before God and man that his fame began to redound in distant cities and countries, like the fame of Achmed the Wise, or that of the one whose name we utter only with the greatest deference, Sheik Ibrahim.

I was filled with admiration for the style in which this tale was written, one that felicitously combined the elegance, grace, and polish of classical tradition with the modern sense for the simple and the monumental. Much as he appealed to me, I had not believed the silverbeard capable of such an accomplishment, and it would have been a great pleasure for me to become better acquainted with him. But unfortunately his artistic temperament must have sensed that his nascent composition was being spied on by the curious, possibly philistine, or even envious eyes of a colleague. Suddenly and forcefully he slammed his notebook shut, and his eyes, full of genius and wisdom, punished me with a look of such unspeakable contempt that shamefacedly and sadly I retreated into myself and left the table before the end of the meal . . .

(Here the manuscript breaks off.)

Christmas with Two
Children's Stories

WHEN OUR QUIET little Christmas celebration had come to an end—it was not quite 10 p.m. on December 24—I was tired enough to look forward to sleeping through the night and especially pleased at the prospect of two whole days without mail or newspapers. Our big living room, the so-called library, looked every bit as disheveled and fatigued as but far more cheerful than we felt inside; for although we had celebrated only as a threesome—master, mistress, and cook—the little Christmas tree with its spent candles, the confusion of colored, gold, and silver papers and ribbons, and on the table the flowers, the stacks of new books, the paintings, watercolors, lithographs, woodcuts, children's drawings, and photographs propped up—some of them erect, some weary and nearly collapsed—against the vases, all this gave the room an unaccustomed, festive air of superabundance and agitation, a touch of the annual fair, of the treasure house, a breath of life and of absurdity, of childishness and playfulness. And the air was charged with scents, as disorganized as they were wanton, the closely mingled scents of resin, wax, scorched things, of baked goods, wine, and flowers. Furthermore, the room and the hour were crowded with the pictures, sounds, and scents of many, very many bygone holidays, to which old people are entitled; since my first grand experience of it, Christmas has returned to me more than seventy times—and if my wife has in her many fewer years and Christmases, it is for that reason that the strangeness, the remoteness, the extinction, and the irretrievability of a sense of home and security were even greater in her than in me. If the last few strenuous days of giving and wrapping gifts, of receiving and unwrapping them, of reflecting on real and imaginary obligations (neglect of the latter often more bitterly takes its revenge than neglect of the former), of the whole somewhat overheated and overly rushed activity of Christmas in our restless age already have taken their toll, then the reencounter with the years and holidays of so many decades has been an even more arduous task. But at least the latter was a genuine and meaningful one, and genuine and meaningful tasks have the virtue of not merely making demands on one and wearing one out, but also of aiding and fortifying one. Especially in a decaying civilization, one that is diseased with a lack of sense and slowly dying, for individuals as well as for the community as a whole, there is no other medicament and nourishment, no other source of strength that enables one to go on, than the encounter with that which, in spite of everything, gives meaning to our lives and our actions and justifies us. And in the recollection of a whole lifetime of holidays and gatherings, in listening to the sounds and stirrings of the

(195

soul—even as far back as the colorful wilderness of childhood, in gazing into beloved eyes long since extinguished,
there is demonstrated the existence of an intelligence, a
unity, a secret center we have circled around—now con-
sciously, now unconsciously—all our lives. From the pious
Christmases of childhood, redolent of wax and honey, in a
world seemingly sane, safe from destruction, incapable of
believing in the possibility of its own destruction, through
all the changes, crises, shocks, and reevaluations of our
private lives and of our age, there still remains a core, a
sense, a grace residing in no dogma of the church or of
science, but in the existence of a center around which even
an imperiled and troubled life can always form itself anew,
from just this innermost core of our being, a belief in the
accessibility of God, in the coincidence of this center with
the presence of God. For where He is present, yes, even
the ugly and apparently meaningless may be borne, because, for Him, seeming and being are one and in-
separable, for Him everything is meaning.

Our tree had long stood dark and a bit foolish on its
little table, for some time the sober electric light had been
burning as on any other evening, when we became aware
of a different kind of brightness at the window. The day
had been alternately clear and overcast; beyond the lake
valley, on the slopes of the mountains, long, drawn-out,
thin white clouds, all at the same altitude, had stood from
time to time; they appeared fixed and immovable, and yet,
whenever one looked out at them again, they had vanished
or had assumed different shapes, and by nightfall it looked

as if we would have no sky at all overnight, that we would be embedded in fog. But while we were busy with our celebration, our tree with its candles, our giving of gifts, and memories which came thicker and faster—outside, a great deal had gone on and run its course. When we became aware of this and turned off the lights in the room, we found that an exceedingly beautiful and mysterious world lay outside, shrouded in great stillness. The narrow valley at our feet was filled with fog, upon whose surface a pale but strong light played. Above this bale of fog, the snow-covered hills and mountains arose, all standing in the same uniformly distributed but strong light. And over all these white tablets, the bare trees and forests and snow-free rock formations were like letters of the alphabet, scrawled by a sharpened quill, numerous mute hieroglyphs and arabesques that concealed secrets. But on high, above all this, a mighty sky—white and opalescent— surged with swarms of clouds through which the full moon shone; a restless and undulating sky ruled by the light of the full moon, and the moon vanished and reappeared amid supernatural veils that dissolved and thickened again; and when the moon won itself a piece of clear sky, it was surrounded by elfin cool iridescent lunar rainbows, whose glistening, gliding series of colors repeated themselves in the rims of the irradiated clouds. Pearly and milky the exquisite light flowed and rippled through the sky, reflected more weakly down below in the fog, swelled and diminished as if alive and breathing.

Before I went to bed I lit the lamp again, cast another

glance at my gift table, and like children who on Christmas Eve take a few of their presents to their rooms and if possible into bed with them, I, too, took a few things with me to have and to hold a little before going to sleep. These were the presents from my grandchildren: from Sibylle, the youngest, a duster; from Simeli a drawing, a farmhouse with a starry sky over it; from Christine two color illustrations for my story about the wolf; from Eva a painting executed with verve and force; and from her ten-year-old brother, Silver, a letter written on his father's typewriter. I took these things up to the study, where I read Silver's letter once again, then I let the things lie there, and fighting heavy weariness I went up the stairs to my bedroom. But I still could not fall asleep for some time, the experiences and images of the evening kept me awake, and my series of thoughts, not to be warded off, ended each time with the letter from my grandson, which read as follows:

Dear Nonno! Now I want to write a little story for you. It is called: For The Dear Lord. Paul was a pious boy. In school he had heard quite a lot about the dear Lord. Now he also wanted to give him something. Paul looked at all his toys but nothing seemed good enough. Then Paul's birthday came. He got a lot of new toys, and among them he saw a thaler. Then he cried out: That's what I'll give to the dear Lord. Paul said: I'll go out to the field, I know a nice place where the dear Lord will see it and come to get it. Paul went to the field. When he got there he saw a little old woman who could not walk without support. He was sorry for her and gave her the thaler. Paul said: Really it was meant for the dear Lord. Many greetings from Silver Hesse.

On that evening I was not successful in conjuring up still another memory, the one my grandson's story reminded me of. Not until the following day did it turn up of its own accord. In my childhood, when I was the same age my grandson is now—that is, ten—I had also once written a story as a present, for my younger sister's birthday. Aside from a few schoolboy's verses, it is the single poetic composition—or shall I say the sole poetic effort— that has been preserved from my childhood years. I myself had not given it a thought for decades; but a few years ago, I don't know on what occasion, this bit of juvenilia was returned to me, presumably by the hand of one of my sisters. And although I could only indistinctly remember it, still it seemed to me that it bore some similarity or kinship to the story which my grandson, some sixty years later, had written for me. But even if I was certain that my childhood story was in my possession, how would I ever find it? All our bureau drawers were chock-full; tied-up portfolios and stacks of letters with addresses that were no longer valid or no longer legible were everywhere; everywhere were handwritten or printed papers saved from years or decades ago, saved because one could not make up one's mind to throw them away, saved out of piety, out of conscientiousness, out of want of energy and decisiveness, out of an exaggerated esteem for the written word— this once "valuable material" which might one day be useful for some new project, saved and enshrined, just as lonely old ladies keep trunks and attics full of large and small boxes where they save letters, pressed flowers, locks of children's hair. Even if all year long one incinerates tons of paper, immense amounts pile up around a man of letters who only seldom has changed his place of residence and who is getting on in years. '

But now I was obsessed by my wish to see that story again, if only to compare it with that of my contemporary colleague Silver, or perhaps to make a copy of it and send it to him as a present in return. I tormented myself and my wife with it for an entire day, and I actually found it in the most unlikely place. The story was written in 1887 in Calw and goes as follows:

THE TWO BROTHERS
[for Marulla]

Once upon a time there was a father who had two sons. One of them was handsome and strong, the other was small and crippled; thus, the bigger despised the smaller. The younger one did not like this at all and so he decided to go wandering in the wide wide world. When he had gone a ways, he met up with a carter, and when he asked the man where he was going, the carter replied that he had to transport the treasures of the dwarfs who lived in a mountain of glass. The little one asked him what he would be paid. The answer was that he would receive a few diamonds in payment. Then the little one also very much wanted to go to the dwarfs. And so he asked the carter if he thought the dwarfs would take him in. The carter said he did not know, but he took the little one with him. Finally they reached the Glass Mountain, and the overseer of the dwarfs paid the carter very well for his trouble and dismissed him. Then he noticed the little one and asked him what he wanted. The little one told him all. The dwarf said he had only to follow him. The dwarfs gladly accepted him and he led a splendid life.

Now, we also want to take a look at the other brother. For a long time, things went well for him at home. But when he got older he had to join the army and go to war. He lost the use of his right arm and had to beg. And so as a poor man he came upon the Glass Mountain and saw a cripple standing there, but he hadn't the faintest notion that the cripple was his brother. The latter, however, recognized him at once and asked what he wanted. "Oh, my good sir, I am so hungry that the least little crust of bread would make me happy." "Come with me," the little one said, and led him into a cave whose walls sparkled with countless diamonds. "You can have a handful of these, if you can get the stones out by yourself," said the cripple. With his one good hand the beggar now tried to pry loose some of the diamonds, but of course he did not succeed. Then the little one said: "Perhaps you have a brother. I'll permit you to let him help you." Then the beggar began to weep and said: "Indeed, I once had a brother, he was small and misshapen like you, but he was so good-natured and kind, he certainly would have helped me, but a long time ago I heartlessly drove him away from me, and it's been a long time since I've known anything of him." Then the little one said: "I am your little brother. No longer need you suffer want, stay with me."

That some similarity or affinity exists between my fairy tale and that of my grandson and colleague certainly is not the erroneous notion of a doting grandfather. The average psychologist would probably interpret the two childish attempts along the following lines. Obviously, each of the two storytellers—the pious boy Paul and the little cripple—identifies with the hero of his story; and each creates for himself a situation of double wish-fulfillment: to begin with, a massive receipt of gifts—be they toys or thalers or a whole mountain full of precious stones—and a secret life among the dwarfs, among his peers and far from the grownups, the adults, the "normal" ones. But, above and beyond this, each of the storytellers devises for his narrator a role of moral glory, a crown of virtue, for each of them compassionately gives his treasure to the poor (which in reality neither the ten-year-old old man nor the ten-year-old youth would have done). This may well be correct; I have nothing against it. But it also seems to me that the wish fulfillment comes to pass in the realm of the imaginary and the playful; at least for myself, I can say that at age ten I was neither a capitalist nor a jewel merchant, and never to my knowledge had I seen a diamond. On the other hand, at that age I was already acquainted with *Grimm's Fairy Tales* and perhaps also with the tale of *Aladdin's Lamp,* and for the child the conception of a mountain of jewels was less a notion of wealth than a dream of unspeakable beauty and magical power. And this time, too, it struck me as strange that the dear Lord was not in my fairy tale, though for me He was presumably more of a reality than He was for my grandson, who had only become curious about Him "in school."

Christmas with Two Children's Stories

What a shame that life is so short and so full of pressing, apparently important and unavoidable duties and problems; some mornings one scarcely dares get out of bed, knowing that one's large desk is already piled high with unfinished business and that twice more in the course of the day the delivery of mail will further increase the height of the stack. Otherwise, it would be nice to play an amusing and contemplative game with the two children's manuscripts. To me, for example, nothing would be more absorbing than a comparative analysis of style and syntax in the two attempts. But our life is not long enough now for such delightful games. And, in the end, perhaps it would not be advisable to influence the development of the sixty-three-years-younger of the two authors through analysis and criticism, words of praise or rebuke. Because, circumstances permitting, something may still become of him, though not of the elder.

The Jackdaw

I T HAS BEEN a long time since, as a returning visitor to
Baden to take the cure, I have gone there with the
expectation of being surprised. The day will come when
the last stretch of the Goldwand will be built over, the
lovely spa park converted into factories, but I will not live
to see this. And yet on this visit, on the ugly, lopsided
bridge to Ennetbaden, a wonderful and charming surprise
awaited me. I am in the habit of allowing myself a few
moments of sheer pleasure each day when I stand on this
bridge—it lies but a few steps from the spa hotel—and
feed the gulls with some small pieces of bread. They are
not at the bridge at all hours of the day, and when they
are there one cannot talk to them. There are times when
they sit in long rows on the roof of the city baths building,
guarding the bridge and waiting for one of the passersby
to stop, take some bread out of his pocket, and throw it
to them. When someone tosses a bit of bread up into the
air, the youthful and acrobatic gulls like to hover over the
head of the bread-thrower as long as they can; one can
watch each one and try to make sure that each gull will
get its turn. Then one is besieged by a deafening roaring
and flashing, a whirling and clattering swarm of feverish
life; beleaguered and wooed, one stands amid a white-gray

winged cloud, out of which, without pause, short, shrill shrieks shoot. But there are always a number of more prudent and less athletic gulls who keep their distance from the tumult and who leisurely cruise down below the bridge and over the streaming waters of the river Limmat, where it is calm and where some piece of bread, having escaped the clutches of the vying acrobats up above, is always sure to fall. At other times of day, there are no gulls here at all. Perhaps they have all gone on an outing together, a school or a club excursion; perhaps they have found an especially rich feeding place farther down the Limmat; in any event, they have all disappeared together. And then there are other hours when, to be sure, the whole flock of gulls is at hand, but they are not sitting on the rooftops or thronging over the head of the feeder; rather, they are swarming and raising a din importantly and excitedly just above the surface of the water a bit downstream. No amount of waving or bread-tossing will help, they don't give a hoot, busy as they are with their bird games, and perhaps their human games: gathering the tribes together, brawling, voting, trading stocks, who knows what else. And even with baskets full of the most delectable morsels you would not be able to draw them away from their uproarious and important transactions and games.

This time when I got to the bridge, seated on the railing was a black bird, a jackdaw of extremely small stature, and when it did not fly away at my nearer approach, I stalked it, more and more slowly inching closer to it, one

---

small step after the other. It showed neither fear nor suspicion, only attentiveness and curiosity; it let me get within a half step of it, surveyed me with its blithe bird eyes, and tilted its powdery gray head to one side, as if to say: "Come now, old man, you certainly do stare!" Indeed, I was staring. This jackdaw was accustomed to having dealings with humans, you could talk to it, and a few people who knew him had already come by and greeted him, saying: "Salut, Jakob." I tried to find out more about him, and since that time I've collected quite a bit of information, all of it contradictory. The main questions remain unanswered: where the bird made its home and how it came to be on intimate terms with human beings. One person told me the bird was tamed and that he belonged to a woman in Ennetbaden. Another said that he roamed freely, wherever it suited him, and sometimes he'd fly into a room through an open window, peck at something edible, or pluck to shreds some knitted garment left lying around. A man from one of the French-speaking cantons, obviously a bird specialist, asserted that this jackdaw belonged to a very rare species, which, as far as he knew, could be found only in the mountains of Fribourg, where it lived in the rocky cliffs.

After that, I would meet the jackdaw Jakob almost every day; now by myself, now with my wife, I would greet him and talk to him. One day my wife was wearing a pair of shoes whose uppers had a pattern cut out of the leather, allowing a bit of stocking to shine through the holes. These shoes, and especially the little islands of hose, in-

The Jackdaw

terested Jakob a great deal; he alit on the ground, and with sparkling eyes he took aim and pecked at them with gusto. Many a time he would sit on my arm or my shoulder and peck at my coat, my collar, my cheek, and my neck, or tear at the brim of my hat. He did not care for bread; still, he would get jealous and sometimes downright angry if you shared it with the gulls in his presence. He accepted and adeptly picked walnuts or peanuts from the hand of the giver. But best of all he liked to peck, pluck, pulverize, and destroy any little thing—a crumpled ball of paper, a cigar stub, a little piece of cardboard or material; he'd put one of his feet on it and rashly and impatiently hack away at it with his beak. And time and again one perceives that he does all this not for his sake alone but on behalf of the onlookers, some of whom always and many of whom often gather around him. For them he hops about on the ground or back and forth on the railing of the bridge, enjoying the crowd; he flutters onto the head or shoulder of one of the members of the audience, alights again on the ground, studies our shoes, and forcefully pecks at them. He takes pleasure in pecking and plucking, tearing and destroying, he does all this with roguish delight; but the members of the audience must also participate, they must admire, laugh, cry out, feel flattered by his show of friendliness, and then again show fear when he pecks at their stockings, hats, and hands.

He has no fear of the gulls, who are twice as large and many times stronger than he; sometimes he flies on high right in their midst. And they let him be. For one thing, he who scarcely touches bread is neither a rival nor a spoilsport; for another, I suppose that they, too, consider him a phenomenon, something rare, enigmatic, and a little bit uncanny. He is alone, belongs to no tribe, follows no customs, obeys no commands, no laws; he has left the tribe of jackdaws, where once he was one among many, and has turned toward the human tribe, which looks on him with astonishment and brings him offerings, and which he serves as a buffoon or a tightrope walker when it suits him; he makes fun of them and yet cannot get enough of their admiration. Between the bright gulls and the motley humans he sits, black, impudent, and alone, the only one of his kind; by destiny or by choice, he has no tribe and no homeland. Audacious and sharp-eyed, he sits watching over the traffic on the bridge, pleased that only a few people rush past inattentive, that the majority stop for a while, often a long while; because of him they remain standing, and gaze at him in astonishment, racking their brains over him, calling him Jakob, and only reluctantly deciding to walk on. He does not take people more seriously than a jackdaw should, and yet he seems unable to do without them.

When I found myself alone with him—and this happened only rarely—I could talk to him a little in a bird language which as a boy and youth I had partly learned from years of intimate discourse with our pet parrot and had partly invented on my own; it consisted of a brief melodic series of notes uttered in a guttural tone. I would bend down toward Jakob and talk things over with him

in a fraternal way in my half-bird dialect; he would throw
back his lovely head; he enjoyed both listening and thinking his own thoughts. But unexpectedly the rogue and the
sprite would come to the fore in him again; he would
alight on my shoulder, dig in his claws, and rapping like
a woodpecker he would hammer his beak into my neck or
cheek, until it was too much for me and I would shrug
myself free, whereupon he would return to the railing,
amused and ready for new games. But at the same time
he would survey the footpath in both directions with hasty
glances, to see if more of the tribe of humans were on the
march and whether there were any new conquests to be
made. He understood his position to a tee, his hold on us
great clumsy animals, his uniqueness and chosenness in
the midst of a strange ungainly people, and he enjoyed it
enormously, tightrope walker and actor, when he found
himself in the thick of a crowd of admiring, moved, or
laughing giants. In me, at least, he had gained favor, and
those times when I came to pay him a visit and did not
find him I was disappointed and sad. My interest in him
was a good deal stronger than in the majority of my
fellow human beings. And much as I esteemed the gulls
and loved their beautiful, wild, fervent expressions of life,
when I stood in their fluttering midst, they were not individuals; they were a flock, a band, and even if I looked
back to examine one of them more closely as an individual,
never again would I recognize him once he had escaped
my field of vision.

I have never learned where and by what means Jakob

was estranged from his tribe and the safe harbor of his anonymity, whether he himself had chosen this extraordinary destiny—as tragic as it was radiant—or whether he had been forced to do so. The latter is more plausible. Presumably he was quite young when perhaps he fell wounded or unfledged from the nest, was found and taken in by people, cared for and raised. And yet our imagination is not always satisfied with the most plausible explanation, it also likes to play with the remote and the sensational, and so I have conceived of two further possibilities beyond the probable one. It is conceivable, or rather, imaginable that this Jakob was a genius who from an early age felt himself to be very different, striving for an abnormal degree of individuality, dreaming of accomplishments, achievements, and honors which were unknown in jackdaw life and the jackdaw tribe, and thus he became an outsider and loner who, like the young man in Schiller's poem,* shunned the coarse company of his companions and wandered about by himself until through some lucky chance the world opened for him a door to the realm of beauty, art, and fame, about which all young geniuses have dreamed since time out of mind.

The other fable I've made up about Jakob is this: Jakob was a ne'er-do-well, a mischiefmaker, a little rascal, which in no way rules out his being a genius. With his impudent attacks and pranks, he had at first bewildered and at

---

* "The Lay of the Bell" ("*Das Lied von der Glocke*," 11.66–69).—Ed.

times delighted his father and mother, siblings and relatives, and finally the whole of his community or colony. From early on, he was considered to be a little devil and a sly fellow, then he became more and more impertinent, and in the end he had so provoked his father's household against him, as well as the neighbors, the tribe, and the government, that he was solemnly excommunicated and, like the scapegoat, driven out into the wilderness. But before he languished away and perished, he came into contact with human beings. Having conquered his natural fear of the clumsy giants, he drew closer to them and joined them, enchanting them with his cheerful disposition and his uniqueness—of which he himself had long been aware. And so he found his way into the city and the world of human beings, and in it a place for himself as a joker, an actor, a main attraction, and a wunderkind. He became what he is today: the darling of a large public, a much sought-after *charmeur*—particularly of elderly ladies and gentlemen, as much a friend to humans as one contemptuous of them, an artist soliloquizing at the podium, an envoy from a strange world—one unknown to clumsy giants, a buffoon for some, a dark admonition for others, laughed at, applauded, loved, admired, pitied, a drama for all, an enigma for the contemplative.

We the contemplative—for doubtless there are many others besides myself—turn our thoughts and conjectures, our impulse to understand the fabulous, not solely toward Jakob's enigmatic lineage and past. His appearance, which so stimulates our imagination, compels us to devote some thought to his future as well. And we do this with some hesitation, with a feeling of resistance and sadness; for the presumable and probable end of our darling will be a violent one. No matter how much we may want to imagine a quiet and natural death for him, something on the order of his dying in the warm room and good care of that legendary lady in Ennetbaden to whom he supposedly "belongs," all probability speaks against it. A creature that has emerged from the freedom of the wild, from a secure place in a community and a tribe, and has fallen into the company of human beings and into civilization, no matter how adeptly he may adapt to the foreign surroundings, no matter how aware he may be of the advantages his unique situation provides, such a creature cannot completely escape the countless dangers concealed in this very situation. The mere thought of all these imaginable dangers— from electric current to being locked up in a room with a cat or dog, or being captured and tormented by cruel little boys—makes one shudder.

There are reports of peoples in olden times who every year chose or drew lots for a king. Then a handsome, nameless, and poor youth, a slave perhaps, would suddenly be clad in splendid robes and raised to the position of king; he would be given a palace or a majestic tent-of-state, servants ready to serve, lovely girls, kitchen, cellar, stable, and orchestra; the whole fairy tale of kingship, power, riches, and pomp would become reality for the chosen one. And so the new ruler would live amidst pomp and circumstance for days, weeks, months, until a year had elapsed. Then he would be tied and bound, taken to the place of execution, and slaughtered.

And it is of this story, which I read once decades ago and whose authenticity I have neither occasion nor desire to verify, this glittering and gruesome story—beautiful as a fairy tale and steeped in death, that I must sometimes think when I observe Jakob, pecking peanuts from ladies' hands, rebuking an overly clumsy child with a blow from his beak, taking an interest in and somewhat patronizingly listening to my parrotlike chatter, or plucking up a paper ball before an enraptured audience, holding it fast with one of his clawed feet—while his capricious head and his bristling gray headfeathers simultaneously appear to express anger and delight.